FERAL NATION

The Divide

ALSO BY SCOTT B. WILLIAMS

The Pulse

Refuge

Voyage After the Collapse

Landfall

Horizons

Enter the Darkness

The Darkness After

Into the River Lands

The Forge of Darkness

The Savage Darkness

Sailing the Apocalypse

On Island Time: Kayaking the Caribbean

ISBN-9781723777301
Cover & interior design: Scott B. Williams
Editor: Michelle Cleveland

FERAL NATION
The Divide

Scott B. Williams
Feral Nation Series Book Four

This one is for Joseph. We will miss you.

One

ERIC BRANSON STUDIED THE scene before him with his night vision monocular as he sat drifting in the Klepper kayak, its matte black hull invisible in the dark shadows of the tall pines standing atop the steep bluffs of the lakeshore. He could clearly see the stolen military gunboat he was looking for, tied up alongside a raft of empty barges moored to the bank at the head of the cove. A man with a rifle slung over his shoulder hurried by it, walking the deck of the adjacent barge with his head down and covered by his jacket hood against the rain. The man was obviously on guard duty, but at the moment appeared more annoyed by the weather than concerned with any possible threat. The cold drizzle Eric had paddled through for nearly two hours showed no sign of letting up, but despite the chill it brought to the night, it was a welcome cloak that along with the darkness, would greatly increase his chance of success.

Several other vessels were tied up in front of and behind the gunboat, the barges apparently serving as a floating dock for the operations ashore. Most of the others were small, outboard-powered runabouts and fishing boats, but there was a large pontoon houseboat among the fleet too, and it was towards that particular vessel that the lone man was walking. A dim light was glowing through its lower level curtains, indicating that the houseboat likely served as a guardhouse of sorts, while the gunboat itself was dark and unoccupied, having no real living quarters, just a pilothouse for the crew. Eric watched as the man boarded the houseboat, where he glanced one more time out to the blackness of the rainy lake before disappearing to the comforts inside.

If this was the extent of security here, Eric knew the first part of his operation would be easier than he expected. This cove on a narrow arm of the big lake was several miles south of the lock and dam at its outflow, and since the occupants controlled that entrance as well as the connecting waterway to the south, it was unlikely they were expecting a threat from the water at this hour on a nasty night such as this. Eric would use their complacency to his full advantage.

He'd planned to leave the kayak some distance away and complete his approach to the former campground by circling around through the woods on foot, but what he'd just seen presented new possibilities that might be far more efficient. He wasn't sure if the man he'd seen was the only one aboard the houseboat or not, but what he *was* sure of was the lack of professionalism on the part of whoever was in charge. It would make getting the information he sought that much easier.

Eric put away the monocular and picked up his paddle again, quietly dipping it in long, steady strokes that would quickly close the gap to the barges. Lieutenant Holton had tried to persuade him to bring one of the soldiers from his post along with him in the kayak, both to help him paddle and to provide back up, but Eric had refused. His chances of success were better alone than with an unknown companion, especially one with no experience in this particular type of operation that was truly Eric's specialty.

He was fortunate to have the kayak available at all. It was perfect for what he had to do tonight and the only reason he did have it was because it was his own boat, the one he'd used for his covert entry back to the U.S. after a drop off from a tanker ship near the Florida coast several weeks prior. He'd only brought it along for the journey up the Mississippi in order to stash it somewhere in case he needed it later, as unlikely as that might be. When he was offered the prospect of a faster means to complete his journey west to Colorado by agreeing to a mission proposed by Lieutenant Holton, Eric immediately knew he could put the kayak to good use. The target was on the shore of a lake that was part of a larger inland navigation system, and since he was going in without the benefit of a squad of fellow SEALs and the more sophisticated delivery systems that had been available to him on those missions, the kayak was better than any other option he had. Besides, Eric only had to use it to cover the last few miles, as the lieutenant had been able to arrange for an airdrop from a helicopter in a different isolated cove on the lake that was far enough away its approach wouldn't be heard. If things went as planned, he would rendezvous with the same helicopter crew at another extraction point at 0400. So far, everything had gone as planned. There'd been no sign of activity near the LZ upon approach, and the pilot hovered low over a gravel beach just long enough for Eric to dump the disassembled kayak and hop out after it. When the UH-72 Lakota had disappeared, and all was quiet again on the lake, Eric had worked quickly to set it up, and then he carefully worked his way along the shoreline, keeping to the shallows and close to cover as he paddled to his objective. But there'd been no sights or sounds of movement on the dark lake other than his own, and he attributed that to the nasty weather, which he hoped would hold until he was finished with what he had to do here.

The final approach to the moored boats would expose him to view if the guard he'd seen or anyone else happened to look in his direction, but Eric doubted that would happen before he reached cover again. With smooth, quiet strokes of his Greenland paddle, he made the crossing in less than ten minutes and reached temporary safety when he slipped under the bow the first barge in the lineup. Just as he'd expected there would be, there was enough space between the landward side of the steel hull and the ten-foot-high clay bank to create a hidden passageway sufficient for his kayak to pass. Eric used it to slip quietly towards the middle of the raft, in the direction of the houseboat. From his low perspective in the seat of the kayak, the bank above him blocked any view of what was ashore here, but Eric knew he would find out soon enough. Rather than waste the remaining hours of darkness sneaking around with no solid intel, he hoped to get the answers he needed through more expedient means.

When he reached the third barge in the line, the one he knew the houseboat was tied to, Eric stopped paddling and grabbed hold of one of the mooring cables, pulling himself to a standing position in the cockpit so that he could get a look around. He was still too low to see over the top of the high bank, but he could hear generators running in the distance somewhere in the darkness beyond the lakeshore. He scanned what he could see of the barge decks with the monocular and seeing nothing that moved, pulled himself aboard, keeping low as he lined the kayak into the narrow gap between the barge he was now aboard and the stern of the next one, where he secured his bow painter to prevent it from drifting out into view of anyone who might happen along.

Lieutenant Holton had provided him with most of what he needed, although Eric sorely missed his personal Glock 19 with its precision trigger work and the Trijicon red dot sight mounted low on a Suarez custom-milled slide. In its place now was a standard issue Beretta M9. The M4 he carried was more or less the same as the 3-round burst model he'd surrendered when he and Shauna and Jonathan had to give up their weapons to get past Simmesport and onto the Mississippi. He had a few hand grenades in case they were needed, as well as some other fun stuff in the kayak that he intended to use before he was done here. But for this first move, crossing the decks of the barge, all he carried was the rifle and pistol and the custom blade that never left his side.

The light was still on inside the cabin of the houseboat, and Eric guessed that even though the sentry wasn't dedicated enough to stand out there all night in the rain, he was probably making the effort to at least stay awake. It was possible too that he had a companion aboard, and maybe they were passing the time with conversation or a deck of cards. Either way, Eric was as careful in calculating the risk as he would be knowing they were seasoned pros. He quietly boarded the houseboat from the barge and then climbed the ladder leading to the upper sun deck where he would be out of the line of sight of anyone exiting the cabin. He didn't have time to wait up there indefinitely, but he wasn't planning to kick the door in either and risk alerting their friends on shore with an action that might result in gunfire. Eric knew the guard he'd seen would come back out after a certain interval to have another look around, but if he waited for that he still wouldn't know whether the man was the only one aboard. For that, it would be best to create a good *reason* for him to come out, a minor diversion of some sort that would draw any occupants outside, preferably not with guns at the ready, but to investigate an unexpected sound that couldn't be ignored.

Looking around at what was available to him, Eric decided that a really big splash would probably do the trick. Such a noise wouldn't automatically be connected with an enemy threat, but if it were big enough, it would arouse curiosity, even if they thought it was just a big fish or some other aquatic creature. Eric sliced through the webbing strap holding them down and freed a stack of metal patio chairs that were stored near the aft end of the deck. He threw the first one so that it hit the water just outboard of the rail near the cabin entrance, quickly following up with a second and third that splashed and sank behind the first. Sure enough, it was only a matter of seconds before he heard the cabin door open, and Eric watched and waited, pressed low on the fiberglass roof out of the line of sight of whoever was about to exit.

He didn't hear voices in reaction to the disturbance, and it was a lone man that came to check it out, probably the same one he'd watched from a distance before his approach. Eric lifted his head just enough to see the guard looking over the rail, rifle in hand now, as he pondered the source of the commotion. The concentric ripples caused by the splashes were still visible but beginning to diminish as the dark waters of the lake once again became calm and quiet. If the man wasn't alone, Eric knew this was the time he might speak out to let whoever was inside know there was nothing to see outside. When he didn't however, and instead moved to step back inside out of the rain, Eric felt sure he was indeed dealing with only one guard. He waited until just before he closed the door, and then he sent another chair sailing over the rail, this one hitting the lake several feet forward, near the bow.

The splash immediately drew the guard back out, and Eric followed him, crouching low on the roof above until his unsuspecting target was exposed on the open forward deck. Setting down the M4 to keep his hands free, Eric leapt quietly to the lower level just behind his quarry, pulling the man down and slamming him to the deck in one smooth motion as he absorbed the momentum of the jump with his legs. The guard's rifle clattered against the rail as they went down together, and Eric helped it over the side with a nudge of his foot. Before he could cry out or struggle, Eric had a hand clasped over his mouth and the point of his big blade bearing against the soft underside of his chin, so that there could be no mistaking that he meant business.

The guard seemed to realize the futility of putting up a fight after being taken down so efficiently and with no warning. His eyes were wide with fear and he nodded and remained quiet when Eric removed his hand from his mouth, believing the warning that he would taste cold steel if he uttered a sound louder than a whisper in answer to the questions that followed. He assured Eric that he was indeed alone on the boat and alone on waterfront guard duty until his watch ended at dawn. Eric searched him for additional weapons, removing a large folding knife clipped in his pocket before securing his wrists behind his back with one of the heavy plastic cable ties he'd brought for the purpose. Then he got the man to his feet and led him aft to the open cabin door. Once inside, Eric forced him to sit before securing his ankles with another cable tie. Then he set about getting the answers to some of the other questions he came here to resolve. He couldn't be sure he was getting the truth, but none of the guard's replies seemed particularly far-fetched.

"It wouldn't have happened, and they'd still be alive if they hadn't come here and started shooting first," the man said when Eric asked him about the gunboat and its missing crew and learned that only the sergeant in command had survived. "They didn't leave the men at the lock any choice. They were under attack."

Eric doubted that part of the story, figuring it was actually the other way around, and that the gunboat crew had been fired on first. "They were here to investigate the closure of the Waterway," he said. "They have federal authority to be here, as do I. Now, I want to know where that sergeant is being held, and if what you tell me isn't the whole truth, I'll be back before I leave to make sure it's the last lie you'll ever tell."

"I'm not lying, man. He's in the compound, but you're crazy if you think you can get him out. You might have gotten the drop on me out here, but you'll never get through our camp perimeter. You'll end up dead just like those other federal thugs."

"We'll see about that," Eric said.

Before he left him, Eric gagged the man so there'd be no chance he would call for help. While it was probably more prudent to finish him then and there with the knife, Eric was here for one purpose and this time it wasn't to kill as many of the enemy as possible. As far as he was concerned this man wasn't his enemy anyway unless he was an active threat, and at this point he no longer was. With the guard unable to sound a warning, Eric wasn't overly concerned about his ability to recon the encampment undetected. Tonight's weather was perfect for that sort of thing. Besides, with the diversion he intended to create soon enough, stealth would be totally irrelevant before he was done here.

Eric quietly exited the cabin of the houseboat and checked the line of barges again before climbing to the roof to retrieve his rifle. Then he made his way back across the adjacent barge to climb back into the cockpit of the kayak, leaving it tied there out of sight in the shadows while he crouched in the seat and pulled out the canvas bags he'd stashed under the decks fore and aft. The explosive charges and remote detonation system inside were sorted and ready to go, he just had to place them into position and so they'd be all set when he was ready for the fireworks.

When he had everything ready and close at hand in the cockpit, Eric paddled out from under the barge and made his way down the outside of the line to the gray steel hull of the gunboat, working quickly to place his magnetic packages on the topsides just below the waterline. Getting out of the lake with the government vessel intact was out of the question with the exits from the lake blocked at both ends by locks, so an essential part of his mission here was to destroy or disable it so that it was no longer available for unauthorized use. He had more than enough C-4 to take care of that, and enough time when he was finished to set about disabling the other boats tied up to the barges by opening any drain plugs he found accessible and removing or slashing their outboard fuel lines.

Finished with those preparations, Eric paddled swiftly to the south along the lakeshore until he was a quarter mile past all the barges, where he secured the kayak beneath a clump of low-hanging bushes growing out from the bank and stepped ashore. He was carrying the M4 and a load-out of spare magazines for it and the Beretta, as well as the hand grenades and the RAMS detonator for the explosives. If the man he'd interrogated was telling the truth about the time of the next watch change, Eric didn't have to worry about anyone finding him on the houseboat before the action started. If he moved quickly there'd be more than enough time to reach his objective and figure out a way to get the sergeant out. The steady rain had fallen long enough to thoroughly soak the ground and the leaf litter of the forest floor, making it easy to quietly wind his way among the trees in a hurry. Eric didn't know what kind of security measures might be in place at the compound but finding just one man watching the waterfront indicated to him that whoever was in charge here had confidence in the remoteness and inaccessibility of this location. Considering that they controlled the lake and no doubt all the roads leading into the area, that was understandable, but nevertheless unprofessional and whoever was responsible would realize his error soon enough.

Fifteen minutes later, Eric had reached the edge of a large, parklike clearing and was scanning the former recreational campground through his night vision monocular. More than a dozen motorhomes and travel trailers occupied the main campsite pads along the loop road, just as one might have observed here most any night before everything changed. But in addition to the recreational vehicles, there were numerous enclosed cargo trailers and even portable buildings of the type normally used for storage sheds or workshops in the backyards of suburban homes. Pickup trucks and SUVs of all descriptions were parked everywhere amongst them, and a tall fence with 6-foot high mesh and several strands of barbed wire above that defined the outer perimeter.

Eric was focused on one particular metal-sided shed that was located near the south side of the cluster, just where the man on the houseboat had told him he'd find it. It was part of the reason he'd approached the campground from that side, and the pair of Rottweilers he saw pacing nearby was the other. The man hadn't been lying about the presence of the dogs, and Eric figured they were the reason for the mesh wire fencing. He was also willing to bet there were more inside the compound than just the two he could see, but with the breeze still out of the north due to the cold front that brought all this rain into the area, Eric was downwind of those sensitive canine noses for now. It was unlikely he'd be detected from where he was watching, but mere observation wasn't going to accomplish what he was now determined to do. Eric had to trust he could pull this off and get it right the first time because he only had one chance and no backup if he failed. He set the detonator control box on the ground next to him as he continued to watch the campground. All hell would break loose as soon as he pressed that activation button, that was a given. Eric just had to make damned sure that's what he wanted to happen when he did it.

Two

"THIS ISN'T A RESCUE mission," Lieutenant Holton had strongly emphasized, when they were studying the maps and discussing Eric's options. "We don't even know if the boat crew is alive or dead. What we *do* know is that these insurgents are in possession of the vessel and that they have already demonstrated hostile intentions by firing at a military aircraft. We know that they have effectively shut down the Tenn-Tom Waterway, but other than that, we don't have a lot of intel on what's going on down there or why. We had our last radio contact with Sergeant Connelly right about *here*, on the river just below the lock and dam at the outflow of this lake." The lieutenant pointed to a large man-made reservoir on the map spread out on the table in front of them.

Eric wasn't familiar with the Tenn-Tom Waterway, other than knowing it was an alternate connection between the Gulf of Mexico and the upper Mississippi and Ohio Rivers, but looking at the entire route now, he could see why it was important, bypassing as it did New Orleans and Baton Rouge, both of which were major trouble spots since the region was hit by the recent hurricane. This lake the lieutenant was showing him was located on the southern border of Tennessee, where the top corners of Mississippi and Alabama met. From there, the Tenn-Tom Waterway led south through a series of smaller lakes, rivers and canals, with several additional locks eventually dropping it to sea level to create a shortcut for barge traffic heading north from Mobile. Much of the route passed through sparsely populated areas, and this particular lake was no exception.

"We don't have the resources, for one thing, not to mention authorization." Lieutenant Holton said when Eric asked why the people who seized control of the area had not been swiftly dealt with by a responding force. "It's completely outside my AO, but since it connects to the rivers here, I'm making it my business anyway. But that's where you come in. We don't even know who these people are or exactly what it is they want. It's not like they're part of a clearly defined insurgency like we're used to dealing with in the usual hotspots overseas. That's why I sent a boat to investigate in the first place. I thought they were just a group of opportunistic bandits stealing fuel and other goods, and that they'd give up or run for it at the first sign of a challenge. We certainly didn't expect them to take on a heavily-armed gunboat crew, but apparently, that's exactly what they did. And then they fired on the helicopter we sent to look for our boat. These people *will* be dealt with in due time, Branson, and dealt with like the terrorists they are, but you've got to understand that there's so much going on everywhere around the country that nothing happens fast enough. My responsibility is to watch over this part of the Mississippi and lower Ohio and keep it open for navigation. But even though the Tenn-Tom is far to the south, what happens there affects us here too. After what happened, we need eyes on the ground, so we'll know exactly what we're dealing with when we move to eliminate the problem. That's why I'm making you the offer we discussed, Branson. This is what you *do*. I know that from the records we were able to pull. Now that Sergeant Connelly and his men are missing in action down there, I don't have anyone else at my disposal that can handle a job like this. Connelly himself was a Ranger way back and he's seen plenty of Special Ops action like you, but he may already be dead for all we know."

"If he and his crew *are* alive, I'll bring him back," Eric said.

"I understand the sentiment, and I know you SEALs never leave a man behind, and all that, but I wouldn't go in there with high expectations of pulling that off if I were you. That crew wouldn't have surrendered their vessel without a fight, but if any of them *are* alive, then sure, it'd be great if you could bring them out. We could certainly get more intel that way because they're bound to have seen and heard a lot if they were being held. I'm just saying that's not the primary objective. I want that gunboat taken out of commission, so they can't use it to further terrorize traffic on that waterway and I want an estimate of the numbers of insurgents we might be dealing with."

"Understood," Eric said, "but one more question: What are the rules of engagement here? It's still hard to wrap my mind around the idea of a combat mission in Tennessee and Mississippi. And besides, I've been working private contracts so long I don't have a clue how things are done by the book these days anyway."

"These days I'm not sure anything's done by the books, but I can tell you that *survival* is the primary rule right now, Branson. Get in there and get back out so that you can report back to me, whatever it takes. Otherwise, your mission is as useless to me as it will be to you and your wife. Do your part and we'll do ours to get you where you want to go when you're done. But understand this, like I said before: this mission is *off* the books and if anybody ever asks, I'll tell them I've never heard of you. You're on your own out there, Branson, so if you screw it up, you've got to own it. If you miss your ride, we're not coming back after your ass. Is that understood?"

"Loud and clear, sir. I know the drill." But Eric also wanted to clarify another thing. He wanted assurance that Shauna and Jonathan wouldn't simply be thrown off the post if he didn't make it back.

"If that were to happen I'll do my best to see that they get where they want to go, but I have every reason to believe you'll be back to go with them. Your record speaks for itself, Branson."

Eric was confident too after hearing everything the lieutenant had to give him on the situation. He certainly didn't come back stateside to engage in this kind of operation, but the reward for pulling this one off was too good to pass up. A flight to Colorado by military aircraft would change everything, saving him and Shauna and Jonathan many days and possibly even weeks in getting where they needed to be to begin looking for Megan. Eric wouldn't have considered doing something like this for hire, nor did he have any intention of re-enlisting to fight more battles after all he'd already given the Navy. The mission was strictly a means to an end for Eric, but he knew going in that if he found that sergeant there and could make it happen, he would do what he could to bring a fellow warrior home.

Now that he was crouching here on the edge of the woods, studying the campground that this group of terrorists or whatever they were had converted into a compound, Eric knew the gunboat captain had survived because the guard he'd interrogated described the prisoner just as the lieutenant had. According to the guard, the rest of the boat crew were killed in the exchange of gunfire that resulted in his capture, and Sergeant Connelly had been wounded too. The guard couldn't tell him how bad, only that he thought it wasn't. Eric didn't know if the former Ranger would be able to move on his own or not, but that didn't deter him. If the man was alive, then he could be saved. If it weren't for those damned dogs he saw wandering around inside the fence, Eric knew he could probably slip in undetected and free the prisoner without a fight. The rainy conditions were perfect for that sort of thing, but no matter how careful he was, Eric knew it would be impossible to get past dogs at such close quarters without raising an alarm. It sucked, but that was simply the way it was.

He would have preferred to get his man out first and on the way to the extraction point in the kayak before setting off the explosives he'd planted. Now, he was going to have to do it before he went in and hope like hell the surprise would create enough confusion to give him a window of opportunity. With any luck at all, most of the armed men in the camp would assume they were under attack and take off towards the lake to look for the source. From what he'd seen so far, Eric doubted they were ready for battle in the middle of the night. Even though some of the men here might be former combat veterans and the security was halfway decent, they likely thought they were isolated enough to be relatively safe.

Eric continued watching with the detonator in hand now, working out the best approach and calculating the time it would take to reach the building where the sergeant was being held. In addition to the two guard dogs that he'd seen first, Eric also determined that there were at least two armed men on watch. They appeared shortly after he settled in to wait, making rounds of the perimeter together, no doubt because they were passing the time by shooting the shit and scarcely concerned about a threat from the surrounding woods on a night like this. They could be easily dealt with, but Eric didn't have the means to quickly silence the dogs, especially working alone, and with armed men to deal with as well. Besides, those Rotts weren't guilty of any wrongdoing, they were simply at the mercy of their idiot owners. Eric waited until the two men were back in view where he could watch their reaction, and then he pressed the button on the transmitter.

The explosive charges were all set to receive the signal on the same frequency and detonate simultaneously. They did so instantly just as they were supposed to, and the sound shattered the still night in an impressive way. Eric watched the two guards spin around in the direction of the lake, fumbling with their rifles, while the dogs cut loose with furious barking and charged in the direction of the sound. Lights flicked on and the sounds of more men yelling filled the air as the echoes of the explosions died away. Eric put away the monocular now, as there was enough light in the compound to see everything he needed to see. Everyone's attention was focused on the lake and the camp was in a near panic. They managed to hold their fire though, and he heard someone shouting orders to spread out and advance towards the shore. Eric took advantage of the confusion at that moment to rush forward to the perimeter fence. He climbed the mesh wire and squeezed under the upper strands of barbed wire, and then keeping low, slipped to the back of the nearest of the metal sheds. From there, it was just a dozen yards to the one in which he expected to find Sergeant Connelly if the guard on the houseboat had been telling the truth.

When a man with a rifle at the ready in both hands stepped into view from the other side of the building, Eric suspected it was indeed the right one. The guard was looking in the direction of all the commotion and like everyone else in the compound, clearly dying to see what was going on down by the lake. Something was preventing him from rushing down there with all his friends to find out, and Eric was sure that what restrained him was strict orders to remain at that particular building, which told him all he needed to know.

The explosions had the desired effect of turning everyone's attention to the waterfront, but the lone guard he was watching wasn't the only obstacle standing in Eric's way. Most of the occupants of the campground had been inside their RVs and asleep, and some were taking longer to get dressed and get outside. Eric didn't have time to wait on them though, because the first ones to rush down to the lake would soon discover there was no enemy to be found there. What they would do then was anybody's guess, but Eric knew he would lose his short window to get in and get the sergeant out if he didn't act immediately and decisively, while the dogs and most of the men were diverted to the waterfront.

The first thing he had to do was take out the guard standing watch by the building. He would deal with any of the late responders if and when they happened to spot him. Keeping low at the corner of the shed behind which he hid, Eric picked a path that would keep him mostly in the shadows while he crossed open ground to the one that held the prisoner. He had his rifle at the ready in case the sentry turned and saw him, but using it would blow his cover and it was a relief that he didn't have to. Eric's diversion had been so unexpected and utterly convincing that no one thought to expect danger from the opposite direction.

Eric rounded the back corner of the larger building and saw that the door was secured from the outside with a heavy sliding bar, but the padlock hanging in the hasp was open, probably because the guard had been inside with the prisoner before the explosions. That was another turn of good fortune because it meant he wouldn't have to stop and search for a key on the guard after he took him out. Although it might have been possible to slip inside behind the man's back, Eric wasn't about to take that chance now. He didn't know how long it might take to get the sergeant out and moving, or if he was even able to move on his own. He had to take down that guard and do it quickly and quietly, so he moved with no further hesitation as soon as he ascertained no one else that might see him was in the immediate vicinity.

Unlike on the houseboat, which was isolated enough from the main camp that it didn't matter, Eric didn't have time to bind and gag this one. Inside the compound, he was at great risk of being discovered if the guard managed to cry out, and he couldn't afford to blow the whole mission by giving him a chance to do so. Besides, after learning that these men had killed the other members of that boat crew, Eric was in no mood for mercy. He slipped up behind him with the big Bowie drawn. He could easily cut the man's throat before he knew what hit him, but Eric knew he might still make some noise, thrashing about as he died, and it would be messy besides. Instead, he dropped him with barely a sound but a dull thud and the slight crunch of bone as the back of his skull caved under the hammer-like blow he delivered with the solid brass of the knife pommel. After scanning his surroundings again to make sure he hadn't been seen, Eric slid back the bar and opened the door of the metal building, leading with the muzzle of his rifle as he stepped inside, sweeping the dark interior of the single room with a compact flashlight held against the forearm of the rifle with his left hand. A shirtless, barefoot man with his hands tied behind his back was staring into the blinding beam, trying desperately to get to his feet, but unable to do so without the use of his hands. Eric glanced down and saw that one of his legs was wrapped in heavy bandages at the knee.

"Sergeant Connelly?"

The man squinted and tried to look again before Eric quickly diverted the beam to one side. "How do you know my name? Who are you?"

"I'm here to get you out. Can you walk?"

"I don't think so. I think my right knee cap is shattered, hit by a pistol round. I can't put any weight on that leg at all."

"Then you'll have to use the other one as much as possible. We've only got a few seconds. We've got to get out of here fast. Where are your boots?"

"I don't know. I haven't seen them since they brought me here."

Eric considered taking the boots off the dead man outside, but there wasn't enough time and they might not fit the sergeant anyway. Sergeant Connelly was going to have to deal with limping on one bare foot until they could get to the kayak, but hell, the man was an Army Ranger, so Eric figured he could handle it."

"Come on," Eric helped him to his feet. "They're going to figure out pretty quickly that there's no one to engage with down at the lakefront. We've got to get out of here before they come back and start looking around. You're the only survivor of your crew?"

"Unfortunately, yes. I lost three good men to these bastards. One gunned down when they captured our boat and the others shot when they brought us here. They were going to kill me too, it was just a matter of time, because I wouldn't talk. I didn't expect the Calvary to show up, but I knew something was up as soon as I heard the blasts. Where's the rest of your unit? Did they set up an ambush?"

"No, there *is* no unit. It's just me. The name's Branson. I'll explain later, let's go!"

Eric put the sergeant's arm over his shoulders, standing next to him on the side of his bad leg. He was going to have to support his weight between every step of his good leg. Thankfully, Sergeant Connelly was a very fit man, probably weighing close to Eric's own 180 pounds. Eric would carry him if it came to that."

"Take this, since you've got a free hand," Eric handed him the Beretta from his holster. "You may need to help me out before we reach that tree line."

Eric carefully opened the door, scanning the parts of the compound in the immediate vicinity before taking the single step down to ground level from the building. He helped the sergeant down and then led the way back around the corner, the way he had approached. No one had noticed the fallen guard and Eric was beginning to think they were home free until he heard a shout and turned to see a man walking rapidly towards them from one of the RVs.

"NATHAN IS THAT YOU? WHERE IN HELL ARE YOU GOING WITH *HIM?*"

The man had a shotgun in his hand, and Eric didn't give him time to figure out that it wasn't his buddy who was helping the prisoner out of the compound. He dropped to a knee, pushing the sergeant against the wall so he wouldn't fall while he put the man down with a single round from the M4.

"Nice work, but I could have handled him with the pistol if you hadn't knocked me off balance," Sergeant Connolly said.

"You'll get another chance to try if we don't hurry. Come on! We've got to move!"

Three

THEY'D JUST MADE IT to the perimeter fence when Sergeant Connelly *did* have his chance to get a piece of the action and a taste of revenge. This time incoming fire rather than a shout was their first warning. The shooters in the compound were at a disadvantage though, blinded by their own lights while firing out into the darkness beyond the perimeter. Eric and Sergeant Connolly had several clear targets and while the sergeant used the Beretta to good effect, Eric emptied most of a magazine from the M4 in a series of 3-round bursts until the incoming was suppressed. Then, he hurled a grenade in the direction of the fallen men before helping Sergeant Connolly clamber over the fence to the outside, where Eric lifted him onto his back and sprinted for the concealment of the trees. He was pretty sure the grenade finished off the shooters that had spotted them, but it would only buy them a few minutes. The rest of the group that had rushed down to the lake would hurry back at the sound of all this new commotion and would quickly discover the dead men and the missing prisoner. Eric wanted to be long gone before they did, and he was counting on them not expecting him to circle back to the lake since they wouldn't have found any sign of their attackers there, other than the destruction of their boats.

Moving through dense woods in the dark with a man unable to walk on his own was anything but easy though. Aside from his shattered knee that prevented him from putting weight on that leg, the sergeant's bare feet were exposed to sharp rocks, briars and any number of hazards that might put his good foot out of commission with a single misstep. There was little option but to carry him, and as soon as they were deep enough into cover to avoid a stray bullet, Eric stopped for a minute to put him down and catch his breath, while laying out his plan to get them out of there.

"I'm sorry I'm slowing you down, Branson. I don't want to be the cause of you getting caught. You can't get me out of here without help. Leave me and I'll go to ground until you can make contact with whatever unit you're with. I can tell you know what you're doing, so I assume they do too. I'll be fine until reinforcements arrive."

"There are no reinforcements coming, and like I said before, there is no unit! I'm working this alone with no support and no authorization. It was supposed to be a recon mission only, but when I found out you were alive, I knew I had to get you out. The only outside help we can expect is a helicopter extraction—if we can make it to the PZ in time."

"If there's an extraction, you must be with some unit somewhere, so who sent you? If it was Lieutenant Holton from our post, then he must have requested help from Special Ops posted elsewhere, because I don't recall ever seeing you around."

"Yes, Holton sent me, and no, you haven't seen me around. I did my Special Ops time in the Navy in another life, but I'm here for my own reasons now, and they have nothing to do with a unit following anyone's orders.

"You were Navy? Which SEAL team? Three?"

Eric didn't answer. "Look, here's the deal. I've got a boat hidden down there at the lakeshore. We'll need it to reach the PZ. I had an alternate overland route to use in case I couldn't use it for some reason, but it's the long way around and it would be pushing to make it in time now even at a run, and you can't even walk." Eric looked at his watch. "The extraction is scheduled for 0400 hours and it's a one-time deal, no do-overs."

"Don't you have a radio you can use to call in alternate coordinates? Surely Lieutenant Holton wouldn't send you out here with no contingency plan."

"That's exactly what he did, Sergeant Connelly, because like I said, this mission is completely off the books and I'm no longer even enlisted. It's a private deal I made with the Lieutenant. I'll tell you more about it later. We've got to move now and get to the boat. I know you can't walk, but maybe you can help me paddle."

"Paddle? You mean like a canoe? Is that the best Lieutenant Holton could come up with? I guess he's being frugal considering he's already lost an armed patrol boat down here."

Eric grinned but it was too dark for the sergeant to notice. "He wouldn't even go that far. I had to bring my own personal boat, but actually, it's a kayak and it's got its advantages. All we've got to do is work our way down to it and then we'll slip out from under them before they figure out what happened. There's still time to make that extraction if we hurry. Let's go!"

Eric half-assisted and half-carried Sergeant Connolly through the dense undergrowth until they caught sight of open water through the foliage. Behind them, in the direction of the campground turned compound, the sounds of men shouting in confusion and anger told them that the empty building and the bodies of the men they'd killed had been discovered. Someone was yelling orders to spread out and shoot anything that moved, and Eric knew they were about to start combing the woods. And just as he and the sergeant reached the top of the steep bank where he'd tied off the kayak, the sound of an outboard motor roaring to life told him that someone had replaced at least one of the fuel lines he'd taken from their other boats.

"That's not a sound I wanted to hear," Eric whispered. "I was hoping we'd be able to get out of this cove and across to the next point to the north before they got a boat running. I didn't have enough C-4 to take out all their smaller runabouts, so I pulled the fuel lines. Someone must have found a spare, so we're going to have to be extra careful. We may be able to stay out of sight by hugging the shoreline, but if we do that, we're going to miss our ride. It's twice as far around with all the little bays and coves."

"Then leave me here with the boat and take the overland route you mentioned. You can make it if you don't delay. I'll be fine."

"Nope, I'm getting you out, one way or the other. If we miss that helicopter, we'll still have the kayak."

Before the sergeant could argue further, they both heard the outboard revving up to speed as the motorboat headed out onto the lake. There was more shouting from the direction of the barges where the rest of the boats were docked, as well as in the woods behind them. It was time to go, but with at least one boat out there looking for the source of the attack, Eric knew they needed to proceed with utmost stealth.

Getting the sergeant down the bank and into the kayak proved almost as difficult as carrying him as far as he already had. Eric had to first climb down himself and get a length of spare rope, and then take it back up with him so he could rig it to lower the injured man to the water's edge. Once there, he was able to manhandle him over the cockpit coaming and into the forward seat. He knew Sergeant Connelly was suffering intense pain throughout all this, but now that he was in the kayak, at least he could keep the weight off his bad leg.

"Give me a paddle, and I'll do my best to help."

"Don't worry about paddling right now. Here, take this instead and keep a sharp lookout." Eric handed him the M4 and his spare mags. "I'll do the paddling for now," he whispered. "All I want to do is ease south along this shoreline to create some distance. The main thing we have to avoid is being seen. Just be ready to shoot if we are."

The other thing they needed to do was cross the cove to the opposite shore so they could head north, but Eric could now see that the boat they'd heard was still buzzing around the cove, the men inside it sweeping the open waters of the lake with flashlights. To make matters worse, Eric heard another outboard fire up from the direction of the barges. He figured that if they'd had time to get two of the boats running, they'd probably also found the man he'd left restrained inside the houseboat. It wouldn't make much difference though, all he could tell them was that he'd been taken down in the dark by a lone attacker—if he would even admit it. Regardless, it was information that would do them little good at this point.

It was going to suck to miss that airlift out, but Eric resigned himself to the fact that it was probably going to happen. He doubted the pilot would hang around long if he didn't get the "all okay" signal Eric was supposed to flash with his light upon his approach. Would he simply turn around and return to the post, or would he spend a few minutes cruising low over the shoreline, giving them a second chance to flag him down? Eric didn't know, but he did know it was the only hope they had of getting that ride, and in this weather, the pilot would have to pass quite close to see anything. The rain was still reducing visibility and when Eric had thought it was just one boat that would be looking for them, he'd considered striking out across the lake on his planned course anyway and simply engaging the searchers when and if they spotted the kayak. Now, with potentially two boatloads of shooters to deal with, that didn't seem prudent, since if they were spotted on open water with no cover the powerboats would have all the advantage with their speed and maneuverability. Eric wouldn't risk it with the wounded sergeant in his care, especially when he knew he could avoid contact by hugging the shore and sticking to the extreme shallows where no one would expect to find a boat.

The shoreline of the cove gradually turned back to the east before it joined the main lake, and Eric's only choice was to follow it and then see whether or not there would be a window of opportunity to make the crossing when they got there. His plan was thwarted, however, when the second boat pulled out from the barges and headed straight for that point at the end of the cove, effectively cutting them off until the men in it decided which way they would go next. Eric eased the matte black kayak into a stand of cattails and came to a stop behind the trunk of a big pine tree that had fallen into the lake when the bank eroded from under its roots. He then slipped out of the cockpit and took the rifle back from Sergeant Connelly, instructing the injured man to lie down in the cockpit out of sight, while he crouched in the shallows just forward of the bow, his head barely above water as he covered the approaching boat with his finger on the trigger.

The boat cruised by at slow speed and the beam of what was probably a 12-volt spotlight swept the shoreline and lit up the fallen tree, but the low-profile kayak was completely hidden behind it and the searchers went by unaware they were mere yards from those they sought. It was a tense few minutes until they were gone, and Eric knew if it hadn't been for the good fortune of being in the vicinity of that tree, he would have had to open fire and take them out. It would have been easy enough to do, but it would renew and intensify the search when the others heard the gunfire. As it was, they would soon be free to move again, as the boat was slowly turning away from shore to follow the first one out into the main lake.

"Now you see why I don't mind paddling," Eric told Sergeant Connelly as he handed him the rifle and climbed back into the cockpit.

"It's a pretty sneaky boat, I've got to admit. I assume this isn't the first time you've used it in this sort of situation."

"No, but I thought I was done with that stuff a long time ago. Turns out you never know though, do you? Who in the hell *are* these guys, and what exactly are they thinking? Have you got any idea?"

"Not really, other than that they hate the federal government and they're taking advantage of the chaos to establish some kind of stronghold out here in the middle of nowhere. Apparently, they picked the Tenn-Tom to take over because it was an easier target than the Mississippi—a lot less traffic but still enough that they were able to commandeer a good supply of fuel from the northbound barges. We don't know the extent of their organization or if there really is one beyond what we know they have along the Waterway. That's what my crew and I were trying to determine. Whoever they are, they've got balls to think they can get away with this. Your one-man operation tonight might give 'em second thoughts though. If they don't find us, they're going to be scratching their heads a long time, trying to figure out who blew up those boats and nabbed me right from under their noses. They thought they were going to break me and get intel about our operations to the north, but they didn't know who they were dealing with or what I've been through before."

Eric contemplated all this as he paddled, quickly getting the kayak up to cruising speed so as to gain as much distance as possible while there was less chance of being seen. The more he learned of what was going on here in the U.S., the more difficult it was to believe. But why he thought his home country was immune to this sort of thing though, he couldn't have said. He'd certainly seen it happening all around him in Europe, and Bart Branson had always said he thought it was all going to unravel here one day like all empires did. Hearing their old man speculate about such things just made Eric and Keith more determined to serve their country, and the two brothers certainly saw their share of combat, just as Bart had in Vietnam. Only Eric made a career of it though. His skills in special operations warfare had been acquired in many different places alongside many different fellow warriors, but he'd never expected to put his specialties to use at home. Sergeant Connelly had apparently been in the middle of all of this madness since it started, and there were lots of questions Eric wanted to ask him, but they would have to wait for now. It was best to paddle in silence, staying alert for any signs of pursuit and as well as the sound of an approaching helicopter just in case there was a chance of getting the pilot's attention.

The buzzing of the two motorboats in the distance provided a steady backdrop to the sounds of their paddle strokes. Once they'd reached open water, Eric had given Sergeant Connelly his spare paddle, and although he wasn't an experienced kayaker, he was able to handle it well enough to help out, even if not enough to make a real difference. The Klepper was one of the most seaworthy kayaks ever designed, but speed was not one of its attributes. It was still miles to the PZ and they still had to stick close enough to shore to be able to duck for cover again if one of the searching boats came back their way. Eric cursed Lieutenant Holton under his breath for not providing a radio with which he could make different arrangements with the pilot, but this wasn't the first time he'd operated this way and he knew the drill. That helicopter would return to the post without them, and no one there would remember a thing about Eric Branson or a kayak, nor would they have a conclusive answer for Shauna. All Eric could hope was that the lieutenant would honor his promise to get her and Jonathan a ride west if he didn't make it.

At 0355, just five minutes before the UH-72 Lakota was scheduled to arrive, Eric and the sergeant were still on the opposite side of the lake, nearly two miles south of the cove that was picked for the PZ. At that same time, they could hear both of the two motorboats returning from a loop further north, and from the sound of it, now turning into that very cove.

"Those bastards are heading straight to the PZ! That helicopter is going to come in right on top of them!" Eric turned the kayak as he cursed, paddling for all he was worth to try and get closer. It was impossible to see anything beyond the glow of the searchlights from that far away though, as the light rain was still falling.

"Listen, I can hear it now!" Sergeant Connelly said.

"Yeah, and they've heard it too. Look! No more lights!"

They listened to the sound of the rotors closing in on the lake but couldn't see either the unlit aircraft or the boats. The only thing visible were small flashes of light near the surface, and Eric knew immediately that the men in the boat were firing on the aircraft, even before they heard the echo of full-auto bursts.

"Sounds like a couple of AKs to me," Sergeant Connelly said. "I hope the gunner could get a fix on those muzzle flashes in this weather. If he did, those assholes are going to wish they didn't make *that* mistake!"

"Gunner? What gunner? There's no M134 or anything like that aboard. It's a Lakota the lieutenant got on loan from a National Guard base somewhere. It's set up for observation and stuff like that. No armament."

"You're shitting me?

"No, but the two extra crewmen that helped me with the kayak were carrying M4s," Eric said. "Maybe they'll at least return fire. I'll bet they're all confused as hell though, running into incoming right where I'm supposed to be."

But though Eric and Sergeant Connelly listened hopefully, they heard no more shooting, only the sound of the rotors receding into the distance as the pilot made a U-turn over the water and sped back the way he came. Eric was pissed that the pilot turned away so quickly without so much as making another pass over the lake, but he knew too that if they'd been low enough when the shooting started, it was possible they could have taken damaging hits even from small arms fire. When the sound faded away to the north, Eric knew for sure the pilot wasn't coming back. He would instead return to the post and report that instead of a kayak, he'd found boats full of armed men waiting in the PZ. Lieutenant Holton would assume Eric's mission was a failure, and that he must have been captured and forced to disclose the time and location of his planned extraction, when in fact it was just dumb luck that the searchers had been there at all.

It sucked because if he'd simply had a radio, all of this could have been avoided, but Eric resigned himself to the way things were, rather than how they should have been. The reality was that he was no closer to reaching his goal of getting to Megan than he was before he met Lieutenant Holton aboard the *C.J. Vaughn,* and maybe even farther from it, in fact. He turned the kayak around to head for the far shore, away from the distant boats, and the two men dug in with their paddles, neither of them talking; both lost in their thoughts of what they were going to do now and how they were going to get back to the base on their own.

Four

ERIC AND SERGEANT CONNELLY finally broke their silence and began discussing their options as they neared the far eastern shore of the lake, opposite the cove where the helicopter had approached. The men in the two motorboats had hung around the area for a while after the pilot turned the aircraft away in the face of their gunfire, but now they had apparently given up. From the sound of their motors, one was heading back in the direction of the compound and the other was going north, likely to inform those controlling the lock and dam of what had happened earlier.

"They won't be back," Eric agreed when Sergeant Connelly said what they both knew—that the two of them were on their own. "That borrowed Lakota is the only helicopter and pilot Lieutenant Holton has available."

"No, after losing the gunboat already, he won't chance it again after he finds out what happened here tonight. He's going to assume your mission failed just like mine."

"Yeah, and that's total bullshit, but it won't be the first time something like this has happened on an operation. I suppose we'll both be written off now."

"I will, along with the rest of my men, but as far as the lieutenant's concerned, you never existed in the first place if what you've told me is true, Branson."

"I've got no reason to lie."

"No, I suppose you don't. You stuck your neck out for me and now you're not getting your end of the bargain any more than Lieutenant Holton is getting his firsthand intel. Now, he'll have to base whatever decision he makes about this place on what he already knows. I know he wants to hit these bastards and take them out, but I doubt he will anytime soon because he doesn't have the resources. The logistics are just too complicated because of the distance unless he can find a way to get more support for it, and that could take a while. It's not like he can call up and ask for another squad of Rangers or SEALS."

"It sounds like a personal problem for the Lieutenant to me and it's out of my hands now," Eric said. "You came here by way of the Tennessee River. How far is it and what's the situation between here and the confluence with the Ohio? It looks like we're gonna have to paddle it."

"If we're going to have to paddle, then it's a long fucking way, that's the situation! But I guess you're right. What other choice do we have?"

46

"From looking at the map with Lieutenant Holton, I remember seeing that the river runs through mostly rural areas; woods and farms and such. Can you confirm that? I've got topo maps of the lake, including the lock and dam area, but nothing of the area downstream, because it wasn't part of the plan."

"There's not much near the river for the most part, that's true. It shouldn't be too hard to stay out of sight, especially traveling at night."

"Did you see any sign of activities below the dam that could be connected to these nut jobs on the lake?"

"Not really. We didn't encounter any hostility until we approached the locks, and even there, everything looked normal from the other side of the dam. The lock gates were open and apparently functioning. We didn't have any reliable intel on what was going on down here, which was the purpose of our investigation. We didn't know that they were in control of this lake too, as the reports we'd gotten were from a bit farther south, on the Tenn-Tom Waterway proper. Once they got us trapped in that lock, there was no escape. I should have known better, but this entire situation is so off the charts that it's impossible to anticipate everything that might happen. Now three good men are dead. It should have been me, instead of them, because I was in command."

"I know how you feel, but you survived, and I think you'll eventually get your opportunity for payback. Lieutenant

Holton is going to want a full debriefing, and a first-hand report from the ground, especially from the inside, is worth a lot. If what you saw of the river is still true, then that dam is the main obstacle we have to worry about. We've got to figure out how to get around it without being seen."

"Well, I'm sure it'd be easy enough on foot, cutting through the woods, but you'd have to go pretty far out of the way. Once they brought me through the lock and onto the lake, I could see that they had camps set up on both ends of the dam. There's a good many houses and cabins on both sides of the lake there too. To go around behind them, you'd have to make a big loop through the hills and then drop back down to the river on the other side. It wouldn't be much of a problem if you didn't have to carry the kayak. You sure don't want a dead weight like me slowing you down! You need to leave me somewhere around here where I can hole up in the woods, and maybe when you make it back and tell him I'm alive, you can talk the lieutenant into sending that bird out here one more time. He'll have no choice if he wants to hear what I've got to report."

"I'm not leaving you behind, Sergeant Connelly, that's settled, and you know it. You don't get to stay here and lay around enjoying a lakeside camping trip while I do all the work to paddle back. I may have to help you when we're out of the boat, but you can still help me paddle when we're on the river. That sounds like a fair trade to me. If we have no choice but a long portage through the hills I can disassemble the kayak and carry it on my back if I have to. I'll make a second trip and carry you too if there's no other way. But first, I want to study all the options."

"Then we'd better pull over to shore somewhere and look at your map. I may not be able to remember all the details I saw that day, considering what had just happened, but the map will help me piece it together."

"We will. Let's take advantage of the dark while we have it though and get a little closer. Once it's daylight I'd like to get a look at the actual dam before we decide what to do. It looks like this rain is set in, so if it holds out and we have to portage the long way through the woods, we can probably get started without waiting for dark again. Once we're on the river, we can switch to moving only at night."

Eric knew the sergeant was right about the difficulty of getting a man who couldn't even walk over a rough portage. Even a short distance would be a lot of work, but if it was too far to carry him, Eric would figure out an alternative. It was going to be a major physical effort and he had already been on the move for hours, but he wasn't ready to rest and wanted to push on if at all possible. That helicopter pilot was returning to the post without him, and after he was debriefed, Lieutenant Holton would have to tell Shauna and Jonathan that Eric was missing. What would happen to them after that, Eric had no idea. The lieutenant had promised he would still help them get to Colorado in the worst-case scenario, but even so, Eric couldn't imagine the two of them going there to look for Megan without him. And even assuming they found her, then what? How would the three of them ever get back to south Louisiana? And how would Eric know if they had or not? This situation was going to complicate the hell out of things, and he had to force himself not to let his thoughts go there and instead keep his focus on relentless forward motion, staying in the moment. He knew he could get back a whole lot faster if he weren't dealing with a wounded man but leaving Sergeant Connelly behind wasn't a consideration. The man was a fellow warrior and one of the good guys as far he knew, and it didn't matter that they'd never met before tonight; Eric was going to bring him out. The trip would take longer, and he'd have to work harder because of it, but Eric Branson was no stranger to setbacks and he'd certainly never been afraid of hard work. He was determined to make the best of the situation and do whatever it took to return to that post and resume his quest.

When dawn finally broke on the lake, Eric steered the kayak towards a narrow sandbar at the base of a steep bank and got out to study the maps. It was time to determine exactly where they were before proceeding any closer to the occupied lock and dam. With Sergeant Connelly's help, the two of them deduced that they were nearing the point where the entire lake made a sharp bend to the west, and just beyond that bend, they would be able to see the dam.

"We can get close enough to get a look without being noticed if we slip quietly up to the tip of this point," Eric said, tracing the proposed route on the map with his finger. The shoreline on the north side of the lake was broken up by numerous indentations and coves, most of the larger ones headed up by creeks flowing from the surrounding hills. Just as Sergeant Connelly had remembered, the map indicated numerous manmade structures and dwellings along the shoreline in the vicinity of the dam and in some of the larger coves. Avoiding them by going around overland would require a long detour farther inland than Eric would have preferred, but there wasn't another reasonable option. Studying the contour lines of the map, he knew it wasn't going to be easy to move both the kayak and a wounded man along that route, aside from the need for stealth.

The only other possibility was to rely on the darkness and bad weather to try and slip by the guards at the dam. That would have been easy enough before the events of last night, but Eric knew they would be on high alert now, after what happened last night. Getting that close in the kayak would be risky regardless of the conditions. Swimming could work, but he wasn't sure Sergeant Connelly was up to that either, and then, they'd have to find another boat on the other side. However they got around it, the dam was going to be a pain in the ass and Eric knew they were looking at many lost hours before they could start down the Tennessee River and be on their way. Even though he was tired, he wanted to go ahead scout both options now, as he was far too restless and anxious to stop now and do nothing.

"Let's paddle on up there where we can get a look at the dam. Then we'll head up into the cove on this side of it and find a place to hide the kayak. You can wait with it while I go check out this power line right of way." Eric pointed to a straight line cutting through the wooded land indicated on the map, running roughly parallel to the lake and north of all the coves. "Following that will be faster than bushwhacking cross-country, but that doesn't mean it'll be easy."

"No, if it's like most power lines in this part of the country, trying to walk it will involve busting through briar patches on the hillsides and wading sloughs and creeks in the hollows. And, we might get shot by a sniper in a deer stand for our trouble."

"Hopefully those clowns at the dam won't be posting lookouts that far away from the lake. At least the rain will reduce visibility enough that we don't have to worry about a really long-range shooter. Anyway, if it looks too iffy, we can always just wait until dark too."

"That looks to be five, probably closer to six miles. That'll take most of a day or night in the shape I'm in, and then you'll still have to come back for the kayak."

"Maybe. I'll know more when I see it first-hand." Eric folded up the map and put it away. They paddled on until they rounded the big bend, all the while keeping as close to the north shore as possible, the kayak hugging the rocks so as not to present a silhouette to anyone looking that way from the dam. "Wait here," Eric said, as he let the boat drift to a stop under a cluster of exposed roots that extended down from a tall sycamore growing right on the edge of the bluff above. "I'm going to climb up there where I can get a better view."

With Sergeant Connelly holding the boat steady against the bank, Eric pulled his way up the wet roots until he reached the base of the tree. From there, he scrambled another twenty feet up the slippery rocks to a narrow ledge from which he had a decent view of the entire west end of the lake. Scanning the shoreline and the dam with his binoculars, Eric could see enough even through the rainy mist to tell that Sergeant Connelly was right. It would be extremely difficult to go any nearer to that dam without being seen. Doing so in the kayak would put them in an exposed position, with little recourse once they were spotted. If he were alone, he might try swimming it at night, but that would require ditching everything but his weapons and finding another boat on the other side. Seeing all the lake cabins he could make out in the distance, Eric had no doubt he could swipe a canoe somewhere on the other side, but he didn't think Sergeant Connelly was up for that kind of aquatic action tonight. He was going to have to make the overland route work, but the idea of acquiring another boat below the dam made that prospect slightly less daunting. Eric carefully climbed back down to tell the sergeant what he was thinking.

"Like you said, it'll take me at least as long to come back and get the kayak as it'll take to get you around there. There's bound to be some unoccupied camps and vacation homes nearby. I'll bet I can locate a canoe on the other side of that dam. It won't be as ideal as the kayak, but it'll work to get us far enough downriver to avoid these folks. Then, we'll see if we can find a motorboat so we can make up for all this lost time."

"I wouldn't count on anything that needs gas, but you're probably right about the canoe. It's your call if you want to leave your kayak. You're the one that has to carry it if you come back for it."

Eric didn't really want to abandon the Klepper, as useful as it was and as impossible to replace as he knew it would be, but he had to consider that every hour lost in the attempt to return to the post increased the chances that Shauna and Jonathan wouldn't be there when he arrived. If it were just the boat he had to portage, that would be one thing. But getting the sergeant several miles through woods and rough terrain was going to be far more difficult. Eric wasn't looking forward to it, but at least if they went that way, they could start now, and not have to wait around all day for darkness to return.

He pushed the kayak away from the bank and turned it around to paddle into the cove just east of the point, following the wooded shoreline until the inlet headed up at the mouth of a small, fast-running stream. After helping Sergeant Connelly out of the cockpit, Eric got out and waded, pulling the kayak a good hundred yards up the shallow creek, where he then dragged it into a thicket to hide it. Then he sorted through the gear he had inside. There wasn't much, since this mission was only supposed to last a few hours. If they could avoid contact, weapons and ammo wouldn't be an issue. He had used all the C-4 and detonators he'd been carrying but he still had four hand grenades and a dozen loaded magazines for both his rifle and pistol. What would be a problem if they didn't find more of soon was *food*. Eric had two MRE's he'd tossed in just for emergencies, but he hadn't expected to need them. Now, he wished he'd taken many more when the lieutenant suggested them. The only other stuff in the kayak was boat-related gear they wouldn't need if he didn't portage the Klepper; a PFD, a small folding anchor, a manual bilge pump and a third take-down paddle.

Leaving the sergeant there with his pistol to guard their stuff, Eric continued on up the creek alone until he came to the place where it intersected the east-west running power line right of way. There was a steep slope rising in either direction from the creek bed, which was to be expected, but there were also old wheel ruts forming a rough road that would be easy enough to follow. Something in the weeds near the edge of the road caught his eye, and Eric walked closer to discover the remains of a deer kill—the head and lower legs of a spike buck—cut off cleanly and unmistakably the work of human hunters. There'd probably been a gut pile too, but the kill appeared to more than a few days old and had already been picked over by scavengers. It would be logical that plenty of hunting was going on here to supplement the supplies of those involved in occupying the dam. The power line right of way was a good place to ambush deer as well as men, but in this rain, Eric felt the risk of using it now was low enough to be acceptable, especially as he didn't see any footprints or wheel tracks in the dirt road that were made since it started.

By the time he returned to where he'd left the sergeant, Eric had worked out a plan for moving his wounded companion. The only thing that was really feasible was to make a travois of sorts, with which he could drag the man behind as he walked. It would be strenuous going, but nothing like trying to carry him on his back. It would also be faster and far more efficient than helping him hobble along on one foot. Eric had what he needed to make such a rig. All he had to do was cut a couple of poles from small saplings for the frame, and then he would remove the tough fabric deck from the Klepper and rig it as a stretcher. He could make a yoke to pull against with one of the spare paddle halves and some lashing line, and that would be that. He figured Sergeant Connelly would object to this proposal though, and he was right.

"You're going to half kill yourself trying to drag me that far. Just help me make a crutch. I may not be able to keep up, but you've been up all night and I haven't. You go on ahead and get some sleep when you get there. I'll eventually catch up."

"Don't be ridiculous," Eric said. "A travois will work great. I can get you there almost as fast as I can walk, and you won't risk messing up that knee even more. Besides, the spare ammo and other stuff can ride with you. We'll do this in one trip unless I'm wrong about finding a canoe when we get there."

"Yeah, if that happens, then you've ruined the kayak."

"Not at all. It won't hurt the deck fabric to use it for this. I'll rig it so that only the ends of the poles touch the ground. It's going to work. You'll see."

Five

THE MAKESHIFT TRAVOIS PROVED better than Eric expected. He had cut two 10-foot support poles from springy hickory saplings that were both lightweight and strong. Pulled from just below waist level, the angle was sufficient to keep the stretcher clear of the ground and the wet mud and rain-slicked leaves of the forest floor decreased the resistance, making it easier to drag and surprisingly quiet. Sergeant Connelly felt better about the situation and gave in to his reluctance at being carried when he saw how well it worked and how much easier it was on Eric than any other method they could devise. He had Eric's M4 cradled across his chest where he could use it quickly or pass it to Eric if necessary. The arrangement kept Eric's hands free to grip the yoke and kept the extra weight off him while he pulled. The downside to the soft ground that made the dragging easy and quiet was that the ends of the poles made two deep and very distinct drag marks that anyone crossing their trail couldn't help but notice. Eric doubted anyone would if the searchers were still looking for signs of their attackers on the lake, but even here, he didn't like leaving such clear evidence of their passing. It would be especially problematic if they didn't find a canoe or some other suitable boat and he had to make a second trip.

"LISTEN!" Sergeant Connelly suddenly whispered. "Is that what I think it is?"

Eric stopped. They were on the power line right of way now, and he'd been slogging up the first long hill, focused on putting one step in front of the other until he made the top of the slope. He was glad to take a break for a few seconds, and as he squatted to set down the travois handles, he heard the unmistakable sound of a helicopter in the distance. It was somewhere to the south, probably making a pass over the lake. *So, they came back to look for him one more time and now he was deep in the woods instead of on the lake!*

"Well, I'll be damned! I didn't expect them to come back again at all, much less in broad daylight!"

"Too bad it won't do us any good out here," Sergeant Connelly said. "Not unless that pilot just happens to circle back over this power line this way on his way out."

"Not likely," Eric said. "I'm sure he'll stay high enough to avoid small arms fire too. Maybe Lieutenant Holton sent him back in the daytime to get a look at the compound, to see if I took out the gunboat or not. I doubt he's really expecting to find me."

"Maybe not, but if we were on the lake we could probably get his attention."

That was true, but it wasn't going to happen now. Even if he left Sergeant Connelly and sprinted back in the direction of the lake, the kayak was disassembled and far from the water. The shoreline there was heavily wooded. Unless he was able to paddle out into open water quickly, like in the next few minutes, there was no hope of being seen by that helicopter crew. Eric listened to it several minutes until it droned away in the distance, and then he picked up the travois and resumed his muddy trudge up the steep hill on which he'd stopped. Even though the arrival of the helicopter didn't change their need to keep moving, Eric thought that it might keep the attention of any searchers focused on the lake, and at least that was a good thing. Eric wanted to take advantage of that and put as much distance behind them as he could. He forced himself to go on until he estimated they were over halfway along the portage route. There was still no sign of recent use on the rough dirt tracks that a four-wheel-drive vehicle might use in drier weather, so Eric decided it would be safe to take a break. He had to at this point, as he was nearing exhaustion from lack of sleep and insufficient fuel for the amount of hard work he was doing. They had to find more food as soon as possible, and it would become a priority after they started down the river, as they were still facing days of travel if they had to paddle the whole way. Eric shared one of the two MREs with Sergeant Connelly, insisting that he eat even though he said he didn't need it since all he had to do was lie there and ride.

"It looks to me like they've kept you on a pretty lean diet already. You don't need to get any weaker. You'll never heal like that."

"This knee isn't going to heal itself no matter what I do. I'll be lucky if I ever walk normal again."

"You're lucky the bullet passed all the way through. You'll recover once you get proper attention. There must be a doctor on the post or an open hospital somewhere in the vicinity," Eric said, telling him how surprised he'd been to find a semi-functional hospital in Lafayette, where on top of all the other problems, they were dealing with an infrastructure devastated by a hurricane. This mention of Louisiana was the first bit of conversation between the two men that was not centered on their immediate predicament. Sergeant Connelly naturally wanted to know more—why Eric had been there, and why he was here now—but as soon as he was done eating, Eric was ready to curl up on the wet ground to get a brief nap. He'd pulled the travois into the concealment of the woods before stopping, and Sergeant Connelly agreed to keep watch and wake him in two hours.

"I'll tell you about it after I get some sleep. It's kind of a long story."

The short two-hour sleep wasn't much, but it was better than nothing. Eric had often functioned with less than two in twenty-four. The mind and body could be trained to do it, but it was seldom a pleasant thing. When the nudge at his shoulder told his abbreviated nap was over, it seemed to Eric he'd just closed his eyes.

"I haven't seen or heard a thing," Sergeant Connelly said when Eric asked. "The rain hasn't let up either, but you didn't seem to mind. I know you must have been wiped out."

It was true that he'd been so tired that sleeping out in the open in it didn't faze him, other than the fact that now he was feeling the chill from inactivity. That would change as soon as he started dragging the travois again, and he didn't want to waste much time getting moving, but Sergeant Connelly insisted on getting the answers to some of his questions, so they talked quietly while getting ready to move out.

"That's a hell of a story, Branson. I see why you let Lieutenant Holton talk you into this operation now. It's too bad it didn't work out better for you. Now I really feel bad about holding you up. You must be sick about missing that extraction."

"It's not the first setback I've run into, and I'm sure it won't be the last. I'll get to Boulder, Sergeant Connelly, but I'm taking you back to that post first so I can hold Lieutenant Holton to his word. If Jonathan and my ex have already left when I get there, I'll just have to catch up with them later. Let's go. I'm ready to move out if you are."

Eric knew from double-checking the topo map that they needed to stay on the power line until they came to a creek in the third deep hollow from where they'd entered the right-of-way. Then they would need to follow that creek downstream until it joined a larger tributary that emptied into the river about a mile below the dam. An hour later, they'd reached this creek, and Eric pulled the travois far enough into the woods to hide it before setting it down and helping Sergeant Connelly up on his good leg so he could hobble around a bit with a paddle for a crutch and stretch.

"I'm going to slip down to the river alone and have a look first," Eric said. They both knew from the map that this last leg of the route was the most dangerous, passing much closer to the men guarding the dam than any other section of their portage. "If there's a canoe to be found, I need to find it in the daylight. If not, I'll be going back for the kayak."

"Take the rifle. You're more likely to need it than I am. If anyone spots me in here, they'll have to be well within handgun range to do it."

It took Eric nearly two hours to reconnoiter the rest of the route to the river and the cabins and camps in the area. He found the larger stream that he knew merged with the main river below the dam and keeping well away from its banks in the cover of the undergrowth, he followed until he finally had a view of the broad Tennessee. The place where he emerged on the riverbank was one big bend below the dam so he couldn't see the structures there, but he could see that the river appeared to be wide open downstream. There were vacation cabins scattered in the woods across the river and just upstream of where he stood, and he could tell by the wood smoke from the chimneys of some that they were occupied. But what really caught his attention was the nearest of them, a deserted looking cabin with no smoke visible and exactly what he'd hoped to find: an old canoe, upside down on sawhorses next to the side of a small shed, and leaning against the wall beside it, two paddles. This particular cabin looked run-down compared to the others, and after studying it for several minutes, looking carefully for signs of a dog or anything else that would interfere with his plan, Eric decided it was indeed abandoned.

The canoe was on the wrong side of the river of course, but the prospect of swimming didn't bother Eric. He would wait until after dark, and once across, it would be easy to slip up to the shed and carry the canoe down to the river, as the cabin was a good hundred yards from its nearest neighbor. Whatever risk and effort it took to procure that canoe would be far less than the effort required to go back and get the kayak and would save hours. Eric made up his mind on the spot that this was the way to go. If he hurried back to get Sergeant Connelly, there would be plenty of time to move him to the river before dark and once he had the boat, they'd have most of the night left to paddle as far from here as possible by dawn.

Eric still wasn't as tired as he knew he should be. The short nap had done him some good, but he was running on adrenalin too, determined to keep going until he and the sergeant were in a place of relative safety before he took a real break. There hadn't been time yet, but he was looking forward to hearing more of what Connelly knew of the wider problems in the region and beyond. Eric didn't know if he could tell him anything that would be helpful in his journey to Colorado, but the more he learned of any part of the country the better. Lieutenant Holton had also promised to fill in some of the blanks for him before he set out after returning to the post, but that could be days away now.

Eric made his way quickly back up along the little creek, still feeling confident that no one was searching for them in the woods yet. That confidence was shattered when he was nearly back to where he'd left the sergeant. A gunshot rang out from up ahead, and Eric knew immediately that it was a pistol. A few seconds later, the first shot was followed by two more, and then there was silence. The shooting seemed to come from the same place, with no return fire, and Eric suspected it was Sergeant Connelly firing the Beretta, but at what? He advanced with the M4 at the ready now as he crept through the trees, taking advantage of natural cover as much as possible as he closed the gap to where he'd left the sergeant. He'd still not seen or heard another sound when he reached a point where he could just make out the travois through the foliage, still laying on the ground where he'd left it near the base of a tree. Eric took a couple of steps towards it until he was stopped in his tracks by a loud whisper:

"Over here, Branson! It's all clear!"

"Connelly!" Eric moved closer, looking for the source of the voice until he spotted Sergeant Connelly leaning against a tree trunk, a scoped hunting rifle in his hands. Not far from his feet was a body sprawled face down in the wet leaves. The camouflaged hunting clothing that the dead man was wearing blended in so well that Eric would have walked right by it if he hadn't seen Connelly standing there first.

"What happened? Was this guy alone?"

"No, there were two of them, the other one was carrying a compound bow, although he may have a pistol on him too, that I didn't see." The sergeant handed Eric the rifle when he stepped closer; it was a Remington 750 in 30.06. "They were hunting, judging by the rabbit the one with the bow had hanging from his belt. But I think they were on the lookout for us too, so they're probably with the insurgents at the lake. They must have seen the skid marks this thing left on the power line road and followed it right here. When they saw no one was on it, I heard one of them tell the other one they needed to split up and beat the bushes. The only reason I was out of sight at the time was that I had hobbled over there to the other side of that big log. That MRE kind of messed up my stomach, empty as it was.

"Anyway, I was lucky to be out of sight when they showed up because from what they were saying, I knew they'd kill me if they saw me. I was hoping they *wouldn't* see me, but this guy was about to walk right on top of me. I had him covered, hoping he'd turn around, but then he spotted me and started raising his rifle to shoot. I dropped him with one round, but the other one was over there on the other side of the creek where I couldn't see him. He couldn't spot me either, down low like I was, but when he heard my shot he must have seen his buddy go down. I caught a glimpse of him running back up along the creek, towards the power line and I managed to get off a couple of rounds, but I don't know if I hit him or not. I haven't heard anything moving, but as wet as the ground is, that doesn't mean anything. If he's not down, he's probably on his way back for help. The only thing he saw was that empty travois, so he had no way of knowing how many of us might be out here."

"I've got to try and catch him," Eric said. "If he makes it back to the lake to tell the others, we're screwed! They'll figure out what we're trying to do, and then it'll be impossible to sneak down the river."

"Yes, go ahead! I doubt he'll be coming back looking for me alone. I'm going to try on this other fellow's boots for size. They look about right to me, and my feet are mighty cold."

Eric nodded before stepping across the little creek and slipping through the trees towards the spot where Sergeant Connelly had last seen the running man. Like the one he'd shot, the sergeant said the second man was also dressed in hunter's camouflage. Eric knew he would be difficult to spot in this gloomy, wet forest if he thought he was being pursued and decided to stop and lie in wait, but he had to balance the need for caution against the need to catch this man if he *didn't* stop. With the M4 at the ready and the selector set to burst mode, he moved as fast as he dared. When he found no one in the area where it should have been if the sergeant's rounds had taken him down, Eric figured they'd both missed. But then as he continued on in the direction of the power line, he saw something smeared on the smooth bark of a small tree that stopped him in his tracks again: *fresh blood!*

From the height of the smear, about five feet above the ground, Eric guessed that the wounded man must have paused to lean against the trunk and that he might have been hit in the shoulder, upper arm or back. There was enough of the blood to convince Eric that the wound was serious, but apparently, it wasn't bad enough to stop the man from moving on. Proceeding much more carefully now, Eric spotted more blood among the leaves here and there as he studied the ground and peered into the undergrowth, looking for movement. He could see the power line opening about a hundred feet further ahead, and figured he'd catch sight of the running man if he got there before he had time to top the first hill on the right of way. If so, his target would be well within rifle range and Eric was confident the chase would end there. But he'd taken just two more steps in that direction when he heard a low zinging sound like a fast-flying insect and felt a sudden rush of air near his face just before something smacked into a tree a few feet behind him. Eric instinctively dropped, then glanced around to look for the source of that last sound and spotted the neon plastic fletching of a hunting arrow, its head buried out of sight in the bark of a large beech tree.

Eric was nearly eye level to the ground now and crawling to get behind the base of another big tree in front of him when he caught a glimpse of movement up ahead. It was subtle and hard to pick out in the low light, but Eric recognized the motion of a hand drawing back a bowstring. His rifle was already pointed in that direction and now he instantly brought his sights into line with the movement he'd seen and squeezed off a succession of 3-round bursts until he was certain there was no longer any threat of being skewered by a broadhead.

Six

"I THINK YOU HIT him in the left upper arm, but it was hard to tell for sure after all the damage from my 5.56 rounds," Eric told Sergeant Connelly, after returning to where he'd left him waiting. "I figure that's the reason he missed me with that arrow, even if not by much, and the reason he couldn't get off another shot before it was too late. He was obviously good with this though," Eric said, setting the bow down beside the travois, along with the gutted carcass of a rabbit nearly decapitated from being struck in the neck with a broadhead. "I think he was trying for the same results with me!"

"I told you they were hunting. I guess they were looking for us at the same time?"

"I imagine. I don't suppose they'd miss an opportunity to add to the larder, especially if they could do it quietly. Anyway, since he already had the rabbit, I didn't want to let it go to waste, considering we've got one MRE left. The meat will keep well enough in this cool weather until we get somewhere we can cook it."

"Are you thinking of doing more hunting? Is that why you brought the bow too?"

"Maybe. It could prove useful in some way. I figured it couldn't hurt to have it." The bow was short and lightweight, and fitted with a compact bow quiver that held six broadhead-tipped, carbon fiber shafts, although the one that nearly hit Eric was missing a point, as he hadn't been able to remove it from the tree it was buried in. The rig was far more high-tech and expensive-looking than anything Eric ever owned, but he and his brother Keith had quite a bit of bowhunting experience. It was simply a natural part of the whole outdoor experience Bart had shared with them as boys.

"I see the boots fit," Eric said. Sergeant Connelly had also taken the dead man's camouflaged hunting jacket. He was going to be a lot more comfortable now, as Eric knew he'd been suffering out here with no shoes or even a shirt. With rain still falling and the air already chilly by late afternoon, his companion would have suffered greatly tonight without this windfall. Out on the riverbank, Eric could feel the bite of the north wind that was building behind the wave of rain as the frontal system moved across the region.

"They're almost perfect, and the jacket didn't even get messed up."

"Face shots are the way to go," Eric said, nodding at the hole just above the bridge of the dead man's nose. By the way, before I heard your shot, I was coming back to tell you I did indeed find a canoe near the river, so as soon as it gets dark I can snag it and we'll start downstream. I think we'd better put some miles behind us without delay because when these two don't show up tonight, it's going to draw a lot of attention to these woods if anyone back at the lake knew where they were hunting. They'll find those drag marks and figure out which way we were heading. I'm going to try and cover our tracks the rest of the way at least. Maybe that will slow them down some."

Eric picked up the travois again and dragged Sergeant Connelly along the stream bed until they were at last within sight of the river, but still hidden in the woods. It wouldn't be dark for another hour, so he backtracked and did his best to obliterate signs of their passage, moving leaves over the skid marks and his own footprints in the most obvious places so that it would be difficult for anyone to follow the trail, especially in the dark. He was sure someone would find the bodies by tomorrow or the next day, but by then he planned to be many miles to the north on the Tennessee.

Stealing the canoe was relatively straightforward. Eric waited a full hour after nightfall, all the while watching the abandoned cabin and the surrounding yard through his night vision monocular until he was certain it was truly unoccupied. When he was satisfied that it was, he moved Sergeant Connelly to a concealed position on the riverbank and gave him the monocular and his M4, then he removed his boots and stripped to make swimming easier, wearing only his belt so that he could carry his knife and the Beretta. It was already chilly in the night air and rain, and the river was colder yet, but the cold was invigorating and gave him the burst of energy he needed as he was already lagging again after so many hours with so little sleep. He reached the far bank a hundred yards or so downstream due to the current and then began picking his way back up through the riverside undergrowth until he was at the edge of the yard, confident that Sergeant Connelly would cover him if anything went wrong.

Nothing was stirring though, so Eric bent low and crossed the yard to the canoe, checking it quickly to make sure the hull was sound before squatting under the yoke and lifting it off the sawhorses and onto his shoulders. With one hand to balance it by a thwart, he grabbed the two paddles with the other and returned to the edge of the yard and then descended the bank down to the river. Ten minutes later, he was pulling it up into the weeds close to where Sergeant Connelly waited, and in another five minutes was dressed and he and the sergeant were off, paddling silently and hugging the bank to keep to the shadows as they quickly put the next bend behind them.

For this particular purpose, the canoe might prove even better than the kayak, Eric thought, as they skimmed quietly along. It was certainly easier to get an injured man in and out of it, and the single-bladed paddles required a far smaller range of motion than a kayak paddle, making it easier to paddle without splashing and less likely that a wet blade would flash a reflection of light that could be seen from a distance. The canoe was faded forest green, so it blended in with the night almost as well as the matte black Klepper. Like the kayak, it could be easily carried far enough into the woods to hike it so that the two of them could stay out of sight every day while waiting for darkness to return.

Eric had no way of knowing if the owner of the cabin and the canoe was in the area, but from what he'd seen of the place, it looked doubtful anyone would miss it. Even so, when the bodies of the two hunters were found, along with whatever the rain left of the drag marks along the power line road, any searchers from the lake might deduce that the Tennessee River was their destination. Eric didn't know how far downstream they might venture to look for them, but he intended to treat the entire journey like an E&E from deep behind enemy lines. He could afford to do no less after all that he'd seen, as unbelievable as it still was that such a thing could actually be happening here in the homeland.

If anyone from the lake thought to look for them on the Tennessee, they weren't doing it tonight, though. Eric and Sergeant Connelly paddled a deserted river through a steady, cold rain until around midnight, when the precipitation finally tapered off and then stopped altogether. The wind was getting stronger out of the north though, and in some of the long, straight stretches of the big river, it made hard work of the paddling. By 0400, Eric decided he'd had enough. He was certain they'd covered a good fifteen miles, maybe closer to twenty, as they'd had some help from the lazy current despite finding headwinds. He did his best to pick a place that looked as unlikely a landing spot as possible. The bank was steep, but once he'd hauled the sergeant up there and hidden the canoe into the woods at the top, it was as if they had effectively vanished from the river. Eric checked to be sure there was no road behind them, and then he practically collapsed with exhaustion, falling into a deep sleep for several hours until an annoying buzz in his ear became so persistent that he couldn't ignore it. He opened his eyes to bright daylight and checked his watch: 0900. Sergeant Connelly was stirring too and was likewise listening to the sound Eric now knew was an outboard motor.

"I'll check it out," Eric said, grabbing his rifle. The boat was approaching from upriver, so Eric quickly moved into position near the top edge of the bank where he could watch from the concealment of the foliage as it went by. When it rounded the bend, he saw that it was an aluminum bass boat and that there were four men aboard, all of them scanning the banks and the river course ahead, clearly searching for something, as the man at the controls maintained a speed of barely 10 miles per hour. The one seated in the forward swivel fishing chair had a rifle in hand, and Eric saw more weapons leaning against one of the bench seats behind him. These men were clearly from the lake they'd left behind and seeing them now confirmed the wisdom of Eric's decision to travel the river only at night. The boat continued on until it rounded the next bend and the sound of its outboard gradually faded away in the distance. How far they would go before turning back was a guess Eric wouldn't bet on, but he figured they were surely looking for whoever attacked the compound. It seemed doubtful that the two bodies in the woods had been discovered already, so it was probably just a follow-up patrol, and they'd likely done the same thing yesterday.

Eric reported what he'd observed to Sergeant Connelly and then curled up on the ground to sleep some more, as he wasn't nearly caught up on all the hours he'd lost. When he woke the next time, it wasn't to a sound but rather a smell that made his stomach growl. When he opened his eyes, he was surprised to see bright afternoon sunlight filtering through the trees overhead. The rain was completely gone, and the skies had cleared up since morning. When he sat up, he saw Sergeant Connelly hunkered down over a small bed of glowing coals, the quartered pieces of the rabbit cooking directly on top of them.

"I'd say it's about ready. I couldn't risk more than a small twig fire and I had to hunt around to find enough dry branches, but I finally got some decent coals after that boat went back upriver a couple of hours ago."

"Are you sure it was the same one? You couldn't see it from here."

"No, but it sounded like the same motor; running at about the same speed and everything. It would make sense that they'd head back for home in time to get there before night. Anyway, I knew the breeze would carry any smoke away from the direction of the river, so I decided to risk it. I don't know about you, but I'm starving. One rabbit's not much, but it'll make that last MRE go a little further."

"It looks good to me, but yeah we're going to have to keep our eyes open for more food. We've still got a lot of paddling to do."

"Well, it's more than 200 miles, probably about 220, counting the stretch on the Ohio, depending on how far we actually got last night. Fighting that headwind, it may not have been as far as we thought."

"We could make more than 20 miles a night with plenty to eat, but that's also assuming steady paddling without running into trouble or having to evade anyone. But even if we were making closer to 30 miles a night the trip would take a week. That's unacceptable. We need a faster boat."

"A faster boat is going to come with its own set of problems though, Branson. You know that. Anything with a motor can be heard coming from a long way off. At the same time, it'll prevent us from hearing anything but our own engine noise. It's one thing when you've got steel plate to duck behind and a Browning M2 mounted on the bow, but I don't have to tell you how vulnerable an open skiff would be. I suggest we continue to keep a low profile for another night or two, and then think about our options from there. Worst case, we'd have to paddle as far as the north end of Kentucky Lake. The locks and dam there are secure. We can radio the base from there and they'll send a boat to pick us up."

"It's still going to take days though," Eric said, "and those are days I don't really have."

"Then you should leave me here like I already said. Cut cross country on foot to the highway and see if you can find a ride of some kind. It might not be easy, but it's possible and it could save you a lot of time."

"I'm not leaving you behind after dragging your ass this far, Sergeant. We'll keep paddling for now and see how it goes, but while we're waiting for it to get dark, it would be great if you would fill me in with everything you know about the fucked-up situation in this country, starting with everything you know about what's going on down back there at that lake. You can't tell me that's just a bunch of local rednecks that decided they no longer wanted to pay their federal income taxes. I don't see rural, independent-minded folks like that coming together to unanimously agree to an organized revolt without damned good reason. Am I wrong? Or are we dealing with something else here?"

By the time the two of them were on the river again, Eric had a somewhat better understanding of the big picture. The violence that had erupted nearly nationwide and almost simultaneously wasn't nearly as random as it appeared at first glance. Although some of it *was* spontaneous and unplanned, Sergeant Connelly assured Eric that there were powerful people and organizations behind the slow build-up to this and that it had started years prior. Nothing was ever completely as it seemed, and the growing divide between citizens of a once united nation had been largely orchestrated by purposeful and carefully planned dissemination of propaganda designed to fuel discontent and anger. Like any fire, when more fuel was added, in this case in the form of seemingly random terror attacks, it spread and grew beyond the control of those who'd first started it. In the vacuum the chaos and confusion created, Sergeant Connelly said there was no shortage of charismatic opportunists able to quickly amass a following in their various locations by simply giving the hopeless something to believe, whether a righteous cause or the promise of greater freedom or easy wealth. So many had become recently dispossessed of the latter in particular that they were desperate enough to do anything to get it back.

"That started with a series of massive cyberattacks," Sergeant Connelly said when Eric asked him what he knew of the economic crash that left so many without access to their financial assets. "Of course, it was part of the plan by those seeking to bring down the republic, and it originated both here and from abroad. Then there was the panic, and the run on the banks, with predictable results. When people realized they couldn't get their hands on their cash, and that even if they could, it was essentially worthless, that's when the real trouble started."

"Just one chain reaction after another," Eric said.

"Who would have thought it possible?"

"My father did, for one. He talked about it ever since my brother and I were little kids. He was a 'Nam vet. He insisted that we acquire the skills he thought we'd need some day. It was all fun and games back then—great stuff for a couple of boys growing up in the south Florida woods and waterways—but it led us both to the careers we chose, and now here we are. I guess the old man knew more than we ever gave him credit for."

Eric went on to tell Sergeant Connelly more details of his story, like how he'd met Jonathan and some of the things that had happened in the parish where Keith was a deputy sheriff. "I wouldn't let the old man come any farther. He wasn't too happy about it, but he knew my brother had his hands full down there too, so there was plenty for him to do to make himself useful."

"Interesting that you brought that kid from Florida all this way though, and that it worked out as well as it did."

"Yeah, Jonathan is all right. Normally, I wouldn't consider taking a civilian into the kind of danger we've already been through, and that no doubt lies ahead, but is he really safer anywhere else? Is anybody? Like the old man, he just wants to do something useful. I can't blame him for that. And since he's already saved my life and Shauna's too, I'd say he's earned the right to be on my team."

Sergeant Connelly didn't have anything much to tell Eric regarding what he might find farther west, other than the same generalizations Lieutenant Holton already provided. They would talk more in the coming days, and Eric knew he might remember something he was forgetting now, but regardless of all that he was glad he'd gotten to that compound in time to get Connelly out before it was too late. Those thugs had threatened to hang him if he didn't give up the classified information they thought he had knowledge of and considering how they'd killed the rest of his crew, Eric had no doubt they would have carried it out soon enough. They were bent on expanding their control of the waterways and were trying to size up the opposition to the north, knowing that security resources were even thinner on the rivers than they were on the secondary roads. Eric still didn't know exactly who they were, but he was glad he'd at least dealt them a small blow and left them guessing, unable to discern who was responsible and wondering what was going to happen next. He still didn't like the idea of having to kill fellow American citizens like the two he and Sergeant Connelly left lying in the woods back there, but those men and the rest in their organization had given up their rights by their actions. Eric wouldn't be here to see to it that they were stopped, but he felt confident that good men like Connelly would prevail in the end.

The winds out of the north continued to work against them most of the second night, but by the time Eric was thinking about their next daytime hideaway, he estimated they'd put another 25 miles behind them. With the skies clear again, they could better see what was ahead as they rounded each bend, but the banks of the river were dark and deserted for the most part. Twice, they'd crossed to the other side of the channel when passing riverside settlements that appeared to be occupied, but as far as they knew, no one was aware of the silent green canoe slipping downriver in the dark. But when they passed the mouth of a good-sized tributary, just inside of which was a dock with several motorboats tied up, Eric stopped paddling and let the canoe drift as he studied it through the monocular. It was 0500, and time to decide where to spend the day.

"That looks like it was some kind of guest fishing camp," he whispered to Sergeant Connelly. "Those boats are numbered, and all have the same logo on the side. I'll bet they're rentals."

"Yeah, but probably not now."

"No, but one might be for sale for the right price." They could both hear a generator running, so it was obvious that the cabin attached to the dock was occupied.

"Maybe, but I don't have a penny to my name, as you can probably imagine considering how you found me. And even if you do, most people aren't taking cash anymore."

"I've got something *way* better than cash. I know it's risky, but I think this is worth a try. Let's paddle back upriver a couple hundred yards and wait for dawn. I'll watch the place and see what's going on and if I don't see anything too shady looking, I'll go see if they'll talk. I think we're far enough from that lake that we don't have to worry that folks around here are affiliated with that bunch. But we won't do it unless you agree. We're in this together."

"I trust you to make the right decision, Branson. You've done great so far and I'm lucky to be here. You've got more at stake than I do, so if this is what you want to do, let's do it."

Seven

"WHERE IN THE HELL did you get those?" Sergeant Connelly whispered when Eric showed him the Krugerrand coins he intended to offer in exchange for a boat.

"I came here prepared," Eric said. "I didn't know everything about what I was going to run into here, but I'd heard rumors of the currency problems. Besides, I've been dealing with this as long as I've been working in Europe, and it's how I usually get paid since I've been contracting there."

"You made a good choice. I suppose gold is still pretty universal."

"They've already come in handy, but of course their value is subjective now. I could care less about exchange rates though, as long as they buy me what I need at a price that seems fair, and right now, I need a faster boat."

Eric had tied the canoe to some bushes at the water's edge out of sight of the camp across the tributary channel. He'd helped Sergeant Connelly into position just before daylight and the two of them watched and waited, giving the occupants inside time to stir and hopefully show themselves before he approached them. The sergeant would cover him from his place of concealment with the M4 if things didn't go well. It was less risky than both of them going in the canoe, and Eric thought a man alone would appear less threatening. He would carry the Beretta concealed under his shirt and leave the ordinary-looking hunting rifle and bow and arrows where they would be visible in the canoe. That way, he wouldn't look like a totally unprepared fool out on a leisurely river jaunt.

Two men emerged from the camp house shortly after dawn, and it was apparent that they were getting ready to go fishing as they unhurriedly loaded tackle into one of the boats while sipping coffee from their stainless mugs. The two looked like they were probably locals, and likely were the owners of the fish camp, which had probably been out of business for months. Eric figured they were living off the river now, a not too difficult task for men with the know-how and the right equipment. When Eric paddled into their view, calling out first so as not to alarm them, he wasn't really surprised when one drew a revolver from his belt and the other turned quickly to get something from the cabin.

"I don't want trouble!" Eric shouted. "I just want to talk!"

Both men were watching him closely now as he closed the gap, the other having returned from the door with a pump shotgun in hand. Neither was pointing a weapon directly at him yet though, so Eric paddled closer to the dock so he could talk in a normal voice. "I'm sure you've got fishing to do. I don't want to hold you up, but I see you must have had a rental fleet here before all the trouble started. I wondered if you'd be interested in selling one of those boats, since you've got so many. I'm not picky, but I need something faster than a canoe."

The two men just laughed at the idea at first, one of them stating that none of their boats were for sale, but Eric persisted long enough to get the chance to flash gold in their eyes just as the first rays of the rising sun illuminated the river and the shiny metal in his hand. As it turned out the men were brothers, and yes, they had run a fishing outfit here before the collapse, and having nowhere better to go, had stayed on, guarding their property and indeed living off the bounty of the river and surrounding woods. When the three of them got down to serious negations, Eric found himself three ounces of gold, one canoe and one Remington Model 750 hunting rifle poorer, but he was now in possession of an 18-foot John boat with a 75-horsepower Mercury on the transom. Along with the boat, the brothers had agreed to provide him with 15 gallons of gasoline, which accounted for half of the value of the trade, considering the scarcity of that particular commodity. Eric calculated that it was enough to complete the journey, but the deal had cleaned him out, leaving him little else with which to barter. Shauna had several more of his coins on her, and that would have to see them through to Colorado and back now because the rest of his stash was in Bart's care aboard the schooner.

Because he and the sergeant were completely out of food too, Eric had asked the two brothers if they had any fish they could spare, seeing several collapsible live fish baskets hanging from the dock. One of them went inside and returned with a small paper bag filled with cold, fried fillets that he said was catfish, and the other pulled a couple of good-sized live ones out of one of the baskets and tossed them into Eric's new boat. Eric hadn't told them about his companion or anything else other than that he had to get downriver. He didn't mention why or how far, and when one of them asked, he just said Kentucky Lake, as that particular reservoir was indeed on the way to the Ohio. Eric figured the less he said the better, and he wasn't surprised at the strange looks he got from the two men when he left their dock heading in the opposite direction.

"Let's get out of here!" Eric said, pulling up to the bank and tying off just long enough to help Sergeant Connelly into the boat.

"I take it they warmed up to the sight of that gold?"

"Of course. It took more of it than I wanted to pay, but I'm thinking this is going to beat the hell out of paddling."

"The motor sounds good."

"There's nothing wrong with it that I can tell, and we should have enough fuel to make it all the way to the post, so no worries there. The main thing we have to worry about is keeping an eye out for trouble, because now like you said, trouble can hear us coming."

"Then why don't you let me take the wheel? I can sit there and steer just as well as I can sit somewhere else doing nothing. That'll free you up to run shotgun from the bow unless you want to get some sleep first and head out later?"

"Sleep first? No thank you! I slept yesterday, and I can sleep again when we get to the post. Here, you can eat breakfast on the way!" Eric said, as he grabbed a handful of greasy fish from the bag and handed the rest to the sergeant. "If we have to stop again before we get there, we'll cook those other two then."

Eric advised Sergeant Connelly to steer wide of the mouth of the tributary when they went by. Sure enough, the two brothers were still standing on the dock drinking coffee and no doubt discussing what to do with their unexpected windfall. Both of them stopped and stared as the boat they'd sold went by, this time in the expected direction, but with two crew instead of one. Eric waved once and then pretended to ignore them. They might be curious, but he doubted they really cared what he was up to now that they had his gold. They had more boats than they could use, but gold could be exchanged for many of the things they no doubt lacked.

When the fish camp fell astern and out of sight around the next bend, Eric didn't give the brothers or the transaction another thought, setting his sights instead on the river ahead. It felt good to be moving fast again, and he was optimistic that they had little to worry about in regard to what they were leaving astern.

That all changed about fifteen miles downriver, when Sergeant Connelly steered wide around a big bend and they entered a long straight stretch of river bounded by cattail marsh on both sides. The next bend was at least a mile ahead, and before they'd gone half that distance, two boats suddenly entered the river from out of the tall cattails just ahead. Eric was reaching for his binoculars and Sergeant Connelly was backing off the throttle when both boats suddenly lit up with high-intensity blue LED flashers. Eric had the M4 in hand but kept it low as he studied the boats. There was no need for the binoculars now, as they were coming fast, spreading apart to cut off any possibility of escape. They looked official, but Eric knew that didn't mean anything these days. Running from them wouldn't work though, as there was nowhere to go, and he knew from first glance both vessels were bigger and more powerful than the former rental boat. If they weren't law enforcement, by the time he knew that for sure it would be too late to do anything about it. Eric knew that and so did Sergeant Connelly, who now put the engine in neutral, letting them drift to a stop as it idled.

"What do you think, Branson? Legit?"

"I hope so because we're screwed if they're not, but it looks to me like those boats are fish and game patrol," Eric said, watching them close in. Both appeared to be nearly identical as if from the same agency or department, every visible surface but the blue lights finished in dark, flat-toned green. Seeing them brought to mind his brother, Keith, still doing his best to patrol his jurisdiction despite the conditions and the lack of backup or infrastructure. Maybe the men in these boats were the same, at least he could hope so. He counted five of them in all, each one at the controls dressed in green fatigues that nearly matched their boats. One of the other men wore a similar uniform of BDUs, but in khaki, while the other two wore jeans, dark brown jackets and matching brown caps. All but the operators were holding either rifles or shotguns, their attention fixed on Eric and Sergeant Connelly. When the boats drew nearer, spreading wide to approach Eric's vessel from either side, he saw that he was right in his guess that they were game warden boats. The black graphics on their topsides read 'wildlife enforcement', and the rigid aluminum T-tops bristled with a variety of antennas. Eric raised one hand and bent slightly at the knees to ease his rifle down in the boat. Then, with both hands clearly empty and semi-raised and a smile on his face, he called out a friendly greeting.

"Shut up and keep those hands where I can see them!" One of the two men wearing the brown jackets said. He was holding a short lever-action carbine with the muzzle in Eric's general direction, though not quite pointed at him yet. This man looked older than his companions and Eric could now see that he had a badge—a star-shaped one like the sheriff's department badge his brother wore—pinned to his jacket lapel. As the boat drew closer, Eric could read the inscription on a separate nameplate above it, identifying him as Sheriff Morgan.

"Is there a problem, Sheriff?"

"There will be if you try to make any sudden moves," the sheriff said, before turning to glare at Sergeant Connelly. "Shut that damned outboard off and get your hands up where I can see them too!"

The other men with the sheriff looked on as he did all the talking. There was little choice but to comply, and Eric assumed they'd been stopped simply because these lawmen happened to be there doing something else when they came along on the river. He hoped it was a routine inspection, triggered simply by the fact that he and Sergeant Connelly were strangers here. But though Eric didn't doubt they were who they appeared to be, that didn't necessarily mean they could be trusted. And he knew some of the things he had in the boat with him were going to be hard to explain regardless. His worries were confirmed when at the sheriff's command, the other man in the brown coat who was his deputy, stepped over into Eric's boat as soon as their vessel was alongside. Motioning for Eric to step back, the deputy bent and picked up the M4 from where Eric had laid it.

"We're just passing through, Sheriff. I understand that you have to keep a watch on river traffic in your jurisdiction, but we have no intention of stopping here or anywhere else on the Tennessee. We're just trying to get out of here."

"Passing through from where, exactly? I already know that you've stopped in my county. And I see you've been fishing," he nodded at the two catfish in the bottom of the boat. My friends here with Fish and Game might want to talk to you about that, but I'm more interested in this boat that came from the Barkley Brother's Fish Camp, just upriver."

Eric knew the sheriff could see the rental logo on the side the boat, and that it probably seemed suspicious. "You're right, Sheriff, it did come from there, but it's not stolen. I bought it from the owners this morning."

"You need to see this, Sheriff," the man who'd picked up the rifle interrupted. "This isn't any civilian AR-15!"

"No, it's not," Sergeant Connelly answered before the sheriff could take the rifle from his deputy. "It's an Army-issue Colt M4, and it came directly from my commander, Lieutenant Holton."

"I'm supposed to believe that you were given this rifle by an Army lieutenant? You don't look like a military man to me, and your buddy here damned sure doesn't."

Eric knew a claim that they were soldiers might seem less than convincing. Sergeant Connelly was dressed in the ill-fitting camo jacket and brown duck boots from the dead hunter. His thinning hair was still short, but he hadn't shaved in two weeks. Eric, on the other hand, was sporting the thick, full beard he'd worn for years and he was in need of a haircut too, at least by regular military standards. Worst of all, they both lacked the one thing the sheriff asked for after Sergeant Connelly stated his name, rank and the regiment he was attached to. That one crucial thing that could back up their story was I.D. If the Sergeant had been carrying any in the first place, and Eric didn't know if he had or not, it had been stripped from him when he was captured and interrogated. Eric had nothing on him at all that could identify him from the beginning of the mission. It was part of the agreement he'd made with Lieutenant Holton to assure deniability if things didn't go as planned and he was captured or killed. And because of this, Eric knew he and the sergeant were both screwed when it came to proving who they were.

"I'm placing you two under arrest," Sheriff Morgan said, before telling the other man in the boat to cuff them both.

"Arresting us for what?" Eric asked.

"Possession of an automatic weapon is all the reason I need, if I even needed a reason, which I don't, considering the circumstances. That alone would get you 15 to 20 in federal prison if there was a court available to prosecute you. But aside from that, you don't have proof of who you are and what you're doing in my county. Not to mention, I know you paid for that boat with foreign gold coins. It seems to me that you two fellows must be funded by a terrorist organization!"

Eric stared back at the sheriff as he processed this revelation. *So that's why these two patrol boats had been lying in wait when they entered this stretch of river!* The two brothers he'd bought the boat from must have had a radio at their camp and must have called the sheriff's department or the game wardens. Was it because of the gold coins or simply the fact that Eric hadn't told them he had a companion before he went back upriver after the transaction was done? Whatever it was, it had interested the sheriff enough to go to the trouble of putting two boats into position to intercept them.

"As a matter of fact, I think you might be affiliated with that bunch of pirates that have taken control of the Tenn-Tom Waterway south of here. We know they've got military-grade weapons that they stole from a National Guard armory in Mississippi."

"The only affiliation we have with *those* terrorists is an attempt to find out what they're up to and shut them down! I can assure you that we're all too familiar with the stolen hardware you speak of, Sheriff," Sergeant Connelly said. "They also commandeered my own patrol vessel and killed three of my men. I would still be their prisoner if not for Branson here, who was sent in by my commanding officer to find out what happened to us."

"Let me get this straight: First, you tell me you're a sergeant in the Army, and now you're saying you were taken prisoner by those people controlling the waterway and then this civilian was sent in by your lieutenant to rescue you single-handed?"

"I know it sounds unlikely, but it's the truth. I've never met Branson here in my life until a couple of days ago, and he's not even currently enlisted, so yes, I guess you could say he's a civilian. But the fact is, this man is a former Navy SEAL who made a career out of operations like the one he just pulled off. He volunteered to help Lieutenant Holton and he damned sure did his job, destroying the captured gunboat and getting me out at the same time. It was a narrow escape, but we thought we were in the clear now. We're trying to get back to my post to give Lieutenant Holton a report. Something *will* be done about those insurgents, Sheriff. It's just a matter of acquiring the right assets and implementing a plan."

"Boy, ole boy, that's one hell of a piece of fiction right there! You two are going to provide solid entertainment to your fellow cellmates when you get to my jail. I'm sure they'll enjoy listening to whatever other bullshit stories you can make up, but I've heard about all I need to hear for now."

"You clearly have access to radio communications that most people don't Sheriff," Sergeant Connelly said. "You can verify my story if you can get in touch with someone at our post. There's surely a way to relay a message if I give you the frequencies. If you ever want to see this river opened back up to commercial traffic, it's essential that I get my report to Lieutenant Holton, so a plan can be implemented. We're on your side here, Sheriff. You *have* to understand that."

Eric saw by the sheriff's expressions that he *didn't* understand it, nor did he care to. His mind was made up, at least for now, and that was that. Eric and Sergeant Connelly were both in handcuffs now and seated in their own boat while the deputy secured at towline to the bow from the warden's patrol boat. No amount of argument was going to convince Sheriff Morgan to release them here and let them go on their way, and Eric knew the best they could hope for was a chance to plead their case again later, to somehow get him to at least look into the matter.

Eric was fuming inside, but he didn't let his emotions show. He hadn't given those two bastards that sold him the boat any reason to make that call, and he'd thought they were well satisfied with the payment. Eric understood that few people trusted strangers in this environment after all that had happened, but he'd thought he'd made a solid deal and it really pissed him off because twenty minutes prior he and Sergeant Connelly were speeding down the river on their way to home base. Eric had been confident of making it back before Shauna and Jonathan gave up on him, but now there was no telling how long this would take to get straightened out, if it ever was. The deputy had, of course, found Eric's leftover grenades too upon further inspection of the boat, and that only added to their appearance as terrorists. This rural Tennessee sheriff could literally lock them up and throw away the key or even have them executed and no one would ever know. Eric was sure such things were happening all over, and he was kicking himself because he now realized he and Sergeant Connelly would have been better off sticking to the canoe and traveling only at night, no matter how long it took. He had let impatience get the better of him, and now he was going to pay the price. Eric thought of little else as he sat there handcuffed in the boat next to Sergeant Connelly, both of them under the guard of the deputy's rifle; and both wondering what would happen next as they were towed away to the uncertain fate awaiting them in some small-town county jail.

Eight

SHAUNA HARTFIELD FELT ALMOST as if she were in a prison, rather than on a military post. She and Jonathan had been essentially confined to one building since they'd arrived here. They each had a small private room and the use of a common area and bathroom nearby, but they weren't given free-run of the rest of the facility due to security reasons. Shauna was taken once to a different building to see a medic, who checked her hand wound and said the healing was progressing normally, but that was the extent of it. Since arriving there and disembarking from the *C.J. Vaughn*, Shauna and Jonathan hadn't seen Lieutenant Holton, but she knew he must be around because he was supposed to be in charge of at least some if not all of the operations here. Whatever he'd worked out with Eric was beyond her need to know, and all she could do was wait for it to be finished so the three of them could get moving again.

Eric had assured her that it would be quick, but Shauna was fast losing her patience after three days of waiting. She'd tried talking to some of the other personnel they came in contact with, but other than friendly greetings and small talk, none of those attempts got her anywhere, and Jonathan reported the same. The two of them passed most of their time talking with each other, and this afternoon was no exception.

"This waiting is driving me insane, Jonathan," Shauna said, as she paced the floor of his small room, which was identical to hers. "I thought I was finally done with that when we got on that boat at Vic's house, but here I am again, still waiting, still wondering and not getting any answers! Eric should have been back by now."

"Yeah, you'd think so, but you know he could have easily gotten delayed. He told me stuff always changes on a mission. He said you've got to be flexible and able to adapt. I'll bet he'll be back soon, but whatever job he had to do, he's gonna make sure he does it right."

"I know things change, Jonathan. I just wish Lieutenant Holton would talk to us. I just hate the not knowing. I have no idea where they sent him or even what this is all about, and I know they're not going to tell us that, but you'd think they'd at least give us *something*… maybe let us know if he finished what he had to do or not. Especially since we're stuck here waiting on him. I had to live with this kind of thing for *years*, Jonathan. I did it until I couldn't take it anymore. I guess this waiting now just brings back all those memories. I shouldn't let it, but I can't help it."

She was aware that Jonathan knew the story because Eric had already told the kid how their marriage had ended and how he'd missed out on a lot of time with their daughter Megan because of his extreme career choices. Shauna didn't want to get into a discussion with Jonathan about all that now, but this new situation brought back a flood of memories that made those difficult years seem like yesterday. She knew she should look at it differently now because she wasn't married to him anymore and this time he was doing whatever dangerous job he had to do for the sake of reaching Megan sooner. He hadn't returned here to pursue his old line of work, but he couldn't leave his past behind either, and so of course, it had followed him here too. Now he was right back out there somewhere in the same sort of situation that had caused so much tension between the two of them before.

Shauna knew that whatever Eric was doing for Lieutenant Holton was simply a means to an end—a way of getting the three of them to Colorado faster than any option they had available to them otherwise. The lieutenant's offer was one Eric found hard to refuse, especially now that they were even more aware of the extent of the dangers that stood between them and their objective. But despite understanding all the whys, Shauna still wished she had more information about it all. Confined like this while the hours dragged by, the waiting was going to drive her nuts.

She knew next to nothing about what was going on either here on the post or with Eric because as soon as Eric had agreed to work with Lieutenant Holton, she and Jonathan had been separated from him for security reasons. Eric had told her beforehand that would probably happen once he was privy to the details of the mission because they weren't taking any chances of a leak, even to her. Eric hadn't told the lieutenant or anyone else that the two of them were divorced, and he'd let them go on believing that Jonathan was a nephew of his as well, as that was the story he'd given to the sergeant in charge of the post at Simmesport. He thought it might help their case if the three of them came across as a tight family unit, and so far, that had proved true. But whatever this special job entailed, it was obviously important enough that they wanted to make sure Eric didn't discuss it before it was finished. In exchange for his cooperation, they were offering Eric and his 'family' a lot in return, and Jonathan reminded Shauna of that, as he tried to help her keep her patience.

"We've just got to remember that the waiting we're doing now will probably be worth it in the end. We're gonna be saving a lot of time this way, not to mention energy. I mean, I'm still down for that bike ride and all if it's what we have to do, but it'll be so much nicer to just fly out to Boulder, you know?"

101

"We don't know that they're going to be flying us there," Shauna reminded him.

"Well, we can hope so though. We don't know that they're not. With Eric being a former Navy SEAL and all, I'll bet they'll give us a ride on a Blackhawk or something. Wouldn't *that* be badass?"

Shauna smiled. Jonathan hadn't lost a bit of his enthusiasm, and the more she was around him, the more she could see why Eric liked him. The kid was eager to learn and eager to help. He had proven his courage and loyalty once again in the fight for the *C.J. Vaughn* and its cargo of fuel barges. If not for Jonathan's early intervention, Shauna knew she and Eric might not have survived that situation at all. She was especially glad he'd come along with them now, otherwise, she would be all alone here, essentially detained in her room on this newly-established military post near the mouth of the Ohio River. Without Jonathan, there would be no one to talk to and speculate with as she waited, and the time would surely pass even slower.

"They may even give us all a ride all the way back down to the schooner at Vic's place after we get Megan. In fact, I'll bet they will, because you know that whatever job they had for Eric, he's going to knock it out of the park for them."

"I have no doubt about that part, but that's a little what I'm afraid of too. When they see what he's capable of, they're not going to be satisfied with letting him go after just one mission. They're going to do everything they can to talk him into staying, whether it's reenlisting or just making him an offer he can't refuse. It always happens wherever he works. I'm afraid of it derailing his plans to take us somewhere away from all this mess on the boat. I'm afraid they're going to convince him to stay here and fight even after we get Megan."

"After everything he's told me, I really doubt they could ever talk him into that, Shauna. He really wants to set sail on that schooner. I could tell how excited he was about it when Bart first showed it to us."

"Things could be different now though, Jonathan. When we left Florida, Eric hadn't had any contact with any military to get the real scoop on the situation. I wouldn't be surprised if this Lieutenant Holton tries to tell him they're starting to get things under control again. I mean, we've already seen that they're in control of parts of the river, even if not all of it. I just hope Eric doesn't get suckered into believing we should just stay here until things settle down. I know that's what Daniel wants to do, but I just don't see how all of this is going to get fixed anytime soon. It could take years, even if all the fighting and violence stopped tomorrow."

"I believe you, especially after all I've seen since I met Eric. But even before that, I knew it was going to get really bad. Back before the hurricane took out the power in south Florida, I was keeping up with the news as much as I could, and I said to myself then that the best place to be was on a boat. Even with my little fishing boat, I could get away from most of the craziness and I could always find a hideout where I could catch plenty to eat—at least until it got stolen. I never even thought about a sailboat though, until Eric came along. I just didn't know anything about them. But now I totally get why that was his plan. I don't think he's going to change his mind about it, Shauna, no matter what that Holton dude tries to tell him. I believe Eric when he said he was done with all that stuff. He said he was back here for one thing, and that was for his family."

"He's a little late for that, Jonathan, but I know he's got good intentions. The main thing is that he's back to find Megan. I'm counting on him to do just that, but this mission worries me because no matter how good he is, anything can happen. I never knew half of what he was doing out there even when we were still married. The not knowing was the hardest part."

"He probably couldn't tell you because it was probably classified. That wasn't his fault."

"I know that. He told me the same thing. I know that when he was a SEAL his platoon could be called up at any time to go anywhere. They were doing all kinds of secret missions during those years and I'm sure very few people know what they were even to this day. But even though I understood all that, it didn't make it any easier on me. Even if

SCOTT B. WILLIAMS

he went missing in action or was killed, I still wouldn't have gotten the whole truth about what happened, and I know it. That's why this situation here is making me so nervous. It's the exact same thing."

She knew Jonathan was trying to make her feel better, but the kid didn't really know what to say. No one else would either, but she just had to vent her frustration. Shauna was right back where she used to be all those years before, even though she was no longer married to Eric Branson. She had a husband and a stepson waiting for her to return, and no doubt that they would be worried and anxious until she did. She hated to put anyone through what Eric had so often put her through, but she couldn't help it. They were as safe there with Keith and Bart as they could be anywhere given the current conditions. Bringing them along hadn't been an option, even if Daniel had wanted to which of course, he hadn't. Shauna felt a little guilty that she didn't really miss him very much at the moment, but the truth was it was nice to have some time away from him. Daniel Hartfield wasn't mentally or physically equipped to deal with what they were all facing, but then neither were most people. Like most everyone else, he wanted to just wake up from this nightmare and find himself back in his old life of comfort and affluence. Daniel still believed that somehow, he would, so he wasn't ready to accept the truth even after what they'd all seen in the last few weeks. Shauna couldn't help him with that any more than he could help her with what she had to do. Daniel would have to cope the best he could, and Shauna had to forge ahead without him. She was grateful that Jonathan had come to help, but Eric was the real key to finding Megan, and she couldn't help wondering what she would do if he didn't come back.

"If Eric's not back tomorrow, I *will* get some answers somewhere," she said as she reached for the door to leave and go back to her quarters. "They can't keep us in the dark like this for days on end, and the truth is, it's been long enough that I'm starting to worry that something may have gone wrong. Eric is as good at what he does as anybody ever could be, but that doesn't mean he's invincible. If he doesn't make it back, I've still got to go on and find Megan. He would expect me to because he would do the same."

"He's probably fine, Shauna, but if he isn't, you can still count on me to help you. I'm not quitting either until we find Megan."

"I appreciate the thought, Jonathan, but that wouldn't make sense. You are in no way obligated to do any of this. We've put you through enough already."

"And it was all my choice. If it weren't for meeting Eric like I did, I would still be hiding out in the mangroves down there in Florida. I could have managed for a while, but I was pretty screwed ever since my boat got stolen. Eric helped me out and gave me some better options. I knew there'd be a price to pay because there always is for anything worthwhile. I'm going to help you, Shauna, whether Eric is with us or not. Besides, I can't stop thinking about seeing the Rockies and fishing in those mountain streams. There's no way I'd turn back now."

Shauna tried to sleep but spent most of the night in restless anxiety. She didn't want to think about the possibility of going on to Colorado without Eric, but she knew she would if she had to, and despite what she'd told Jonathan, she'd be grateful for his company if it actually came to that. She wasn't going to give the waiting even one more day though. Tomorrow, first thing, she intended to get serious about getting some answers, and she was going to demand to see Lieutenant Holton. At this point, she didn't care anymore that she and Jonathan were in a touchy situation. Without Eric, they had nothing to offer the lieutenant and aside from his promise to Eric, he was under no real obligation to help them or even allow them to stay here. Pushing the issue might jeopardize their situation, but at this point, she didn't care. If they *were* going to have to go west without Eric, then they needed to get started soon.

Whatever it was that Lieutenant Holton asked Eric to do, Shauna knew that it was of high value to them, and she also knew that they had reason to believe Eric could accomplish the task better than anyone else at their disposal. She knew enough about special operations from what Eric had been able to tell over the years that many such missions were organized and completed without official sanction so that they could be denied if things didn't go as planned. This had to be just such a mission, otherwise, it would have been easier to find a team or individual still in active service than to recruit Eric by making him an offer he couldn't refuse.

She just hoped that after all those years of fighting for his country and for others as a contractor, this wouldn't be the one time his luck ran out. She had faith in him, but there was simply no way of knowing what he was up against or what kind of backup he would have if any at all. She knew she'd never get a straight answer about that out of the lieutenant, whether Eric came back or not, but she would ask him to honor his agreement to help them reach Boulder. As far as she knew, that promise wasn't contingent on Eric's successful completion of his assigned task, but rather his agreement to go in the first place. She hadn't had an opportunity to discuss it with him after that first day though, so she knew there could be surprises. In the worst-case scenario, they would simply have to go ahead with their original plan. All of their gear for the journey was stored here, including the bikes, but of course, they'd had to surrender their weapons to the sergeant in command of the post at Simmesport. Whether Lieutenant Holton would offer replacements was yet another unknown, but she expected that he would in the event that Eric was successful.

Exhaustion finally overcame her sometime in the wee hours of the morning, and Shauna fell asleep despite her worries. She was jarred out of it by a loud knocking on her door though, and when she looked at her watch, she saw that it was 0700, still early, but later than she'd planned to sleep. She opened the door to find a soldier outside, waiting to escort her to a meeting.

"Lieutenant Holton would like to see you in his office. I will take you there now if you're ready to go."

Shauna was surprised but readily complied. At last, she was going to get her answers. "Sure, just let me put on my shoes. Did you wake my nephew, Jonathan? He'll want to go with us."

"The lieutenant asked me to bring Eric Branson's wife. He didn't mention anything about a nephew. You may tell your nephew where you're going if you hurry, but he'll have to wait here, I'm afraid."

Nine

"WHAT DO YOU MEAN you don't know where he is?" Shauna asked Lieutenant Holton. "How could you not know where he is when you're the one who sent him to do whatever it was he agreed to do for you?"

"Your husband failed to make the prearranged extraction," Mrs. Branson. "Since he wasn't where he was supposed to be, the helicopter pilot couldn't pick him up."

Shauna didn't bother to correct the man regarding her last name. No one here had asked to see an I.D. and Eric had referred to her as his wife, rather an 'ex'. As far as she was concerned, they could go on believing it, because that way they were more likely to help her, especially now that Eric was apparently missing. "Did the pilot even bother to look around nearby? Surely Eric was simply delayed by something beyond his control. Where was he supposed to be anyway?"

"I'm afraid I can't give you any details of the mission, other than to tell you that your husband knew going in that it was dangerous. Our pilot encountered hostile forces in the location of the pickup zone. The helicopter was fired on and weather conditions at the time did not permit a further search of the area. We assume that whoever did the shooting got the information on the extraction location from your husband."

"Hostile forces? What kind of situation did you send Eric into? I know there's a lot going on, but you make this sound like the kind of combat missions he used to be involved in overseas."

"It's not all that different, ma'am. Your husband wasn't sent anywhere specifically to engage in combat though. It was a reconnaissance mission, I can tell you that much. I know he's good at that sort of thing, but it's still dangerous when it involves close proximity to the enemy. We don't know exactly what happened or why. I didn't want to keep you in the dark any longer, though so I'm telling you what I can share."

"It's been four days now. Didn't you send someone back to look for him? You can't just leave him out there."

"We *did* send the helicopter back the next day for an overflight of the area, but once again, the pilot couldn't get too close. This area is held by a group of what we think are terrorists and we don't know their capabilities. A shoulder-fired missile could easily bring down a low-flying aircraft. The pilot looked as best he could, but there was no sign or signal from your husband. We have to assume he is missing in action. I'm sorry, Mrs. Branson."

"I wouldn't assume anything about Eric Branson, if I were you, Lieutenant Holton. This isn't the first time he didn't show up where or when he was supposed to. If Eric missed that helicopter, then he had good reason to, but Eric is a *survivor!* He's determined to find our daughter, and he wouldn't do anything stupid that would prevent him from doing that. He will find a way back here, helicopter ride or no, but I feel like I deserve to be given at least some idea where he was. I mean, did you send him halfway across the country, or is it somewhere in the near vicinity? I don't know what kind of helicopter you have but I know some of the ones Eric has flown into combat before have a really long range."

"This one doesn't, Mrs. Branson. He was operating in the region, though not in the immediate vicinity. If he somehow survived and evaded capture, then yes, there's a chance he'll find a way back on his own. I just wanted you to be advised of the situation and let you know that the operation didn't go as planned and that you need to consider your options for the future."

"Are you saying that my nephew and I are going to be kicked off the post now since Eric's mission didn't work out?"

"No, not at all. Not now anyway. Of course, you can't stay here indefinitely, but you don't have to leave immediately either."

"We don't want to stay indefinitely, believe me. In fact, if Eric's not back soon, we will be expecting you to honor the agreement he made with you. The one where you said you'd still see to it that the two of us got a ride to Colorado if something happened to Eric. Will you, Lieutenant Holton?"

"My word is good, Mrs. Branson, although I would advise you two to return to Louisiana instead. Your husband said his brother and father were there, and that his brother is a sheriff's deputy. You'd be safer staying put with family than you will out on the road. I can get you a ride, probably in a supply convoy, but I can't do anything else for you once you get there. You'll be on your own."

"We were on our own before we met you, Lieutenant Holton. We had Eric, and I believe he'll be back, but he understood that I was going to continue on without him, just as he would if something happened to me."

"I won't try to convince you not to, I'm just offering my opinion, based on the intel I have about the situation. You might find what you're looking for and make it out just fine, who can say? In the meantime, you and your nephew can stay here a few more days if that's what you want to do. If we find out anything about your husband or he shows up, of course, you'll be the first to know."

Shauna's mind was racing as she followed the soldier that led her back to her quarters. This was exactly what she'd feared when Eric told her he'd agreed to participate in some kind of secret 'mission' for Lieutenant Holton. She knew military resources were limited from what Eric had told her and from what she'd already seen from Florida to Louisiana and all the way to here. Whatever they'd sent him to do, they'd failed to provide proper support and Eric had paid the price. There was no use getting bent out of shape about it in front of the lieutenant though because it had been Eric's choice to go and he was experienced enough to know what he was getting himself into. She wasn't going to dwell on that now. All she could do was hope for the best, that he would show up soon despite missing his extraction and that they could be on their way as planned. But she knew too she had to start thinking about the possibility that she would be going west alone with Jonathan. It was no longer idle speculation; they needed to discuss it for real. She hated to drag the kid into this, but it was his choice to come along and like Eric, he didn't seem to like taking no for an answer. The first thing she had to do was break the news about Eric to him. She didn't have to knock on his door, because he was waiting for her outside of hers when she reached the building.

"Oh man, that's messed up! You mean they just left him there? What a bunch of dumbasses! Eric would never leave a man behind. I know he wouldn't! We've got to find him, Shauna!"

"We can't find him. We can't even look for him because we have no idea where to start, and Lieutenant Holton isn't going to tell us. All he would say was that it was in the 'region'. That could mean anything."

"I'll bet it's on the river somewhere. That's what this base here is all about, just like that small one back down there at Simmesport. That lieutenant is in charge of security on this part of the river, and he probably sent Eric to take care of some kind of problem somewhere around here."

"Wherever it is, we're not going to find out, and even if we knew, we probably couldn't find Eric."

"So, what are we supposed to do? Just sit here and stare at these walls and wait? This is crazy!"

"We wait until he gets back, or until we decide he's not coming back or they decide we have to go. Those are the only choices we have, Jonathan. I don't like it any more than you do, and I'm really worried about Eric now, after what the lieutenant told me. I don't want to think about it, but we already discussed this before, last night. There's a real possibility Eric's not coming back, Jonathan. I've got to face that and figure out how to go on if he doesn't."

"You mean 'we' have to figure that out."

Shauna smiled back at him. She knew Jonathan wasn't going to back out, and truthfully, she was glad to hear him confirm it. Even if he was still okay, she had a gut feeling that Eric *wouldn't* be back in time after what Lieutenant Holton had told her, so going on without him seemed more likely than not. "The good news is that the lieutenant is apparently willing to honor his promise to Eric. He said he would see that we got a ride to Colorado, even though he strongly suggested that we go back to Louisiana instead. I said no to that, of course."

"Did you ask him what kind of ride?"

"It won't be a Blackhawk, that's for sure. He said something about getting us a ride with a convoy. So, a truck, I suppose."

"That sucks, but I guess it beats riding bikes. I'm still betting on Eric though. He'll make it back before we have to leave. I know he will. He's one badass dude. You know that too, Shauna."

Shauna didn't give up hope that Jonathan was right, but another long day of waiting brought no news. She passed some of the hours sleeping, catching up from staying awake the entire night before, but the result of that was that she was once again wired when darkness fell and so spent another night pacing the floor, worrying and thinking. Although she had portrayed total confidence to Lieutenant Holton and to Jonathan when she said nothing would stop her from going on to Colorado with or without Eric, the prospect of actually doing so was quite daunting. Until he showed up at Bart's place in Florida, Shauna was stuck there, with no reasonable means to even begin to try and reach Megan. Eric had figured out a way, and he'd gotten them out of some tight spots because of his skills and experience. Shauna didn't know how she would do the same without him, or what she would do even if she found Megan. Getting back to Keith's place where Daniel and Andrew waited might be impossible. A ride with a military convoy would guarantee that she and Jonathan would reach Colorado, but the lieutenant couldn't promise them a ride back. Shauna had been so preoccupied with what the officer was telling her about Eric's mission that she hadn't even asked him for any details of what this convoy was all about or what the situation was out in the western regions. She would do so next time she spoke with him, but she hoped the purpose of their next meeting would be to inform her that Eric was back or that they'd at least heard from him. But three more agonizing days passed before the lieutenant finally summoned her to that second meeting, this time inviting Jonathan to join them as well. After all that waiting with no more word, Shauna was still hoping for good news until she saw the look on Lieutenant Holton's face.

"I'm afraid I don't have anything new to report regarding your husband, Mrs. Branson. We have to assume by now that we won't."

"How can you say that? How do you know he's not on his way back as we speak? Was he really so nearby that you can be sure that he's had enough time to get here?"

"We can't be sure of anything, but it's not like we didn't look into it further. I can't give you any details of the operation, but I can tell you that it involved a river and boats.

If your husband evaded the insurgents that were the focus of the mission, his logical return route would be along that river. We sent another boat almost to the area of operation, but the crew didn't see any sign of him, even along the most likely evasion route."

"Maybe that's because Eric didn't want them to see him," Jonathan said. "Maybe he thought it was an enemy boat when he heard it coming. If he did, they'd never know he was there. The dude's a SEAL, man... I mean *sir!* Sorry!"

Lieutenant Holton gave Jonathan a slight smile. "We know what your uncle is capable of, son. That's why I offered him this opportunity to begin with. But despite one's experience and training, a lot can go wrong on such operations."

"I don't understand why you didn't have a better backup plan in place," Shauna said. "Eric ran into that a lot after he started doing private contracting, but I doubt he expected that here, working with the Army."

"He understood the risks and the unofficial nature of the operation, Mrs. Branson. As you are well aware, U.S. military resources are stretched beyond the limit both abroad and at home. What's happening here is completely unprecedented and unfortunately beyond our ability to contain at all times and places. I'm just telling you the facts without leading you along into false hope, ma'am. Your husband may indeed make it back here, but we have no further intel on the situation."

"Why can't you just bomb the shit out of the bad guys?" Jonathan asked. "What could they do against that?"

"It's not quite that simple, son. Aside from not having any bombers readily available for me to call in, there are rules of engagement that even now must be followed. It's even touchier here than elsewhere because these insurgents are American citizens. It's not like we are officially at war with them, we're mainly trying to contain the problem and restore order. But what we're facing is a widespread insurrection probably funded by foreign terrorist organizations and perpetrated by many different factions, some working together, others in direct opposition. It's quite complicated to sort it all out and deal with it. The best I can do is carry out my orders to secure my area of operation. Eric's mission was barely within that area and the problem extends well beyond the location from which he disappeared. We were hoping he would return with good intel from the ground that we could use in the near future, but as it stands, we're back to square one and there's little I can do in regard to that.

"But I *can* do the other thing I promised, and that's why I wanted to talk to you today. If you're still determined to go west to Colorado, there's an opportunity to do so if you're willing to leave as early as the day after tomorrow."

"The day after tomorrow? That's sooner than I expected," Shauna said. "I'm not sure we're giving Eric enough time. Maybe we should wait a few more days."

"Personally, I think it *has* been enough time, knowing what I know about the mission and the situation. If he wasn't captured or killed, more than a week would be enough time for him to find a way back here."

"Not if he's wounded or something," Jonathan said.

"Maybe not, but here's the deal. There isn't a lot of interstate transport going on right now. Most military movements are localized within small regions. I can get you out there in two or three stages, but you can't miss the first one if you want to go. A westbound convoy will be passing not far to the north of here on Thursday, and I can get you on it, but beyond that, I can't really help you. It may be weeks before there's another opportunity if there's one at all, and you simply cannot stay here that long. I'd be in trouble enough if the right people found out you were ever here at all."

"And what about this 'mission' you sent my husband to do," Lieutenant Holton? What kind of trouble would you be in if that were to get out?"

"That's why it was unofficial, Mrs. Branson. There's no record that it happened. Your husband understood that when he agreed to do it, and I believe you understood it too. It wouldn't do you or anyone else any good to mention it again. Now, do you want to go to Colorado or not?"

Shauna and Jonathan spent the rest of the day discussing their options, which they now knew were few indeed. Shauna knew if she wanted to carry on with her quest to find Megan, she couldn't afford to miss that ride, and she knew too that Eric would want her to do exactly that. She still wasn't ready to accept that something had finally happened to him, but did it make sense to keep waiting and hoping that it didn't? If Eric was alive and wasn't captured, he would find his way back here at some point and the lieutenant would tell him they had gone on. It seemed to her the only reasonable thing to do.

Her reluctance to leave without him, hoping up until the last minute that he would prove the lieutenant wrong seemed to make the time pass far faster than before, and the day of their departure was upon them. Lieutenant Holton sent for her and Jonathan one last time, and once they were inside and he'd closed the door, he handed Shauna two envelopes: one containing a signed letter and other paperwork from him and the other one a large padded mailer that she found much heavier than expected when she took it from his hand.

"Show the papers to any soldiers or officers that might question you. It states that you're the widow of one of my own officers who was killed in action, which is a slightly better explanation for this trip than the full truth. Keep the other one sealed and out of sight in your bags. You shouldn't be searched once you're cleared to join the first convoy, and one of my sergeants will escort you far enough to see to that. Before he left, your husband asked me to make sure you weren't unarmed if things came to this and he didn't make it back. He said you knew your way around a Glock 19, so that's what I found for you. It's well used but serviceable. You'll find a half dozen loaded mags in there with it. I hope you don't need them, but I'm not betting you won't."

"Thank you, Lieutenant Holton. Having it will certainly make me feel better."

Jonathan was about to open his mouth, but Shauna cut him off, knowing the kid was going to complain that he wasn't getting one too. The gift of the pistol was an unexpected surprise, and Shauna knew the lieutenant didn't have to do it and could probably get in real trouble for it, especially since serious attempts were being made to disarm civilians everywhere. While it would be nice if she and Jonathan were both armed, and with rifles yet, Shauna knew better than to push her luck. Jonathan got the message and the two of them were dismissed without further ado.

Ten

BEFORE SHAUNA AND JONATHAN left the base, Lieutenant Holton explained that their trip to Colorado would involve two or three separate legs, as there was no one convoy that could take them all the way out there in one shot. The lieutenant explained that due to the vastness of the road network in the U.S., it was impossible to secure and control the secondary or even all of the main routes. As a result, the major interstates were the primary corridors currently in use by the military and Homeland Security and keeping them open required a network of temporary posts and checkpoints at regular intervals with ongoing supply convoys operating between them to provide support. Lieutenant Holton said that she and Jonathan could make their way through this network with the paperwork he had given them, but he couldn't guarantee that there wouldn't be delays along the way. Even so, it would be much faster and far safer than attempting to ride that distance alone on their bicycles. He suggested they carry the bikes with them though, as they would probably need them once they were on their own

123

again. "I'll add the bikes and all your gear to the list in my permission request. It shouldn't be a problem to put them on one of the trucks."

Their journey began with a ride north from the post with a sergeant and several soldiers in two Humvees. The destination was a checkpoint near the river port at St. Louis, where the first convoy would be loading fuel to carry west on Interstate 64. Despite her impatience to get moving again, once they were actually on the road Shauna felt a sickening fear inside her; fear for what may have happened to Eric, and fear of what she and Jonathan might be facing without his expertise and experience. Under escort of these soldiers fully prepared for battle, she couldn't ignore the reality of the dangers they faced out here, where even these heavily armed men were at risk by simply driving them to meet the convoy. She was grateful for what they were doing though and knew Lieutenant Holton was really sticking his neck out to keep his word to Eric.

She knew now that she might never learn the truth about her ex-husband's failed mission unless Eric somehow survived to tell her himself. Whether it went wrong because of faulty planning and lack of intel or simply because of circumstances beyond his control was impossible to say, unless the lieutenant was flat out lying to her. At this point, all she could do was carry on with what she had to do regardless, but when she found Megan she would have to give her the bad news. Her father came back for her, all the way from Europe when he learned of the situation here, but now he was missing in action in what had become a war zone in the very heart of America.

It was a surreal thought, but that it really *was* that bad was obvious now that she was seeing the countryside from the highway for the first time since leaving Florida. The shoulders of the road were littered with abandoned vehicles, pushed out of the lanes after they ran out of fuel. Most looked like they'd been broken into, doors and trunk lids left open to the elements, the owners unlikely to ever come back to claim them. Gas stations and fast food establishments built up around once-busy intersections were empty and unlit, many of them damaged by fire and all of them broken into and cleaned out by looters. Here and there, the two Humvees passed small groups of civilian travelers, some of them walking down the highway in small groups and others riding bikes as she and Jonathan would be doing if not for Eric's sacrifice. Seeing those people out in the open like that, exposed and vulnerable in that desolate landscape, Shauna realized just how scary that must be. Even on the gravel backroads route that Eric had learned of from Keith, they would surely encounter desperate people who might do anything to survive just a few more days.

Shauna knew that after they found Megan they would still be facing the prospect of such a journey, at least if they ever wanted to get back to Louisiana, where Daniel and Andrew and Keith and Bart waited. She didn't know what else they could do but try to get there though. But she also knew that even if they did that without Eric, it was unlikely they'd be able to carry out his plan to sail to some distant island or country these troubles couldn't reach. All of that was too far in the future to think about now anyway though, and besides, it all depended on finding Megan first. Lieutenant Holton confirmed that there were reports of widespread rioting in Denver, just as Shauna had heard even when she was still in south Florida, before the hurricane hit. She didn't know for sure about Boulder, but since so many of the riots started at university campuses, she feared the worst. Now that she was actually on her way there, Shauna suddenly realized how daunting the search for Megan might be. What if there was no one there at the campus at all, or even in the dorms and student apartment complexes nearby?

"You said Megan always had lots of friends," Jonathan said, when Shauna voiced these thoughts as they sat there together on the ride. "I'll bet she made plenty of new ones from around the area since she's been out there so long. The locals would probably know where to go and what to do to avoid problems. I'll bet she's staying somewhere nearby with some friends. Maybe she's up in the mountains in some cool little cabin."

"I hope so, but I don't know how we'll ever find her if she is unless she left something at her apartment that'll give us a clue."

"There'll be something, I bet. And if not, we'll ask anybody that might have known her if they know anything. Somebody's bound to know where she is."

"I've already thought about all of that, believe me, but my biggest worry is that we won't find anybody to ask. I mean, look around you! What happened to all these people who left their cars on the side of the road?"

"Maybe they made it home some other way, or maybe they're in a refugee camp."

Shauna knew Jonathan didn't know what to say and she didn't want to keep on endlessly expressing her worries, as there was little point. They rode in silence the rest of the way until they reached the checkpoint where they were to join the convoy. The trucks weren't ready to roll yet, but the sergeant in charge of her escort reassured Shauna that he and his men would remain until she and Jonathan were cleared to join it, as per Lieutenant Holton's orders. Shauna saw that most of the trucks were pulling tanker trailers that she assumed would be carrying either diesel fuel or gasoline offloaded from the river barges docked nearby. There were also some enclosed trailers with unknown contents, as well as armed Humvees and a troop transport vehicle in which she and Jonathan were eventually seated after their bikes and gear were stored elsewhere. The convoy commander seemed accommodating enough and was expecting them after receiving word by radio earlier. He offered his condolences to Shauna after reading the letter from Lieutenant Holton and assured her that she and Jonathan would safely reach their destination. When they were finally moving again, the ride was noisy and slow, with numerous stops at other checkpoints, some of which involved considerable delays for reasons that she and Jonathan could only guess.

"It looks like they've got this entire interstate pretty much under control," Jonathan said. "I doubt any of those terrorist groups would be dumb enough to try anything here."

"I hope not, but you never know. A convoy carrying fuel is a tempting target, just like the barges on the river."

"They're stupid for not putting soldiers on those too, instead of private security guards like those three that tried to hijack the *C.J. Vaughn*. I'll bet they'll rethink that decision now."

"Maybe. It just depends on whether they have enough troops to go around for all that. It looks to me like they're concentrating their efforts more up here for some reason. There sure wasn't any sign of military presence down on Interstate 10."

"Probably because the hurricane wiped out so much down there nobody cares about it right now. That's what

Keith said, but maybe eventually they'll get around to securing it too."

Shauna knew no one here would tell them if they asked, so she said little to anyone other than Jonathan. She knew the less she did to get noticed the better and playing the part of the grieving widow protected her from any unwanted attention from the men in the convoy. She and Jonathan were sitting alone together on a small bench seat of the truck where they could keep their conversation hushed for now. They had been told this ride would only take them as far as Fort Riley, a major base near Interstate 70 and west of Kansas City. There would be an overnight wait at that base before they switched to different transport for the next leg. The wait turned out to be a full day as well as a night though, and they were assigned shared quarters while there. The idea of waiting again even for that short amount of time was frustrating, but Shauna kept telling herself that they were already much closer to Colorado and that it would all be worth it. Shauna was feeling good thinking about that the next morning when two soldiers came to inform them it was time to go. Jonathan had just stepped out to go to the bathroom, and she told them he would be back in a few minutes and that they would be ready.

"No problem. We need a minute anyway. We have to inspect your bags."

"What for?" Shauna asked, her optimism about getting on the road again turning to dread. "We were cleared when we joined the first convoy the day before yesterday."

"I have my orders, ma'am. That is all."

Shauna watched as the two of them opened the packs and other small bags she and Jonathan had been carrying. She wondered what was taking the kid so long and wished he was here to help her explain, because just as she was afraid it would, the surprising weight of the large padded envelope in her daypack invited extra scrutiny. The soldier that found it handed it to his companion, who likewise surprised at its heft, shook it and squeezed it in several places until his fingers felt enough of the outline of the object inside to prompt him to tear it open without further hesitation.

"Where did you get this? You can't have this on the base!" the soldier glared at her, as he examined the Glock and the six loaded magazines in the envelope with it.

"It was my husband's personal weapon. His commanding officer secured it for me after he was killed in action recently. He knew my husband would want me to have it, and that my nephew and I might need it for protection once we arrive at our destination in Colorado. It was sealed in there for the trip because I had no intention of even looking at it while we were here. I know it's not permitted, but my bag hasn't been out of my sight since we joined the convoy at St. Louis."

"I'm sorry for your loss, ma'am, but I have orders to confiscate any unauthorized firearms regardless of the circumstances. You're not allowed to have this on the convoy to Fort Carson or here on the base."

"Please!" Shauna said, "You've got to understand how much that pistol means to me! It's the only thing of his I have left! I promise it'll never come out of that envelope until we are off of the convoy and away from all military operations. I have to look for my daughter when we arrive in Boulder, and I have no idea what dangers we'll face out there."

The soldier was unmoved by her pleading as his companion finished the inspection of the other bags. Jonathan still hadn't returned, and Shauna knew she would lose their only weapon if she didn't act fast. There was possibly a way to make these men change their mind, but if she was wrong, she could end up in more serious trouble and never join that convoy at all. Shauna decided it was worth the risk. These soldiers were human after all, and as such, they were susceptible to the right kind of temptation.

"Wait! I have something else you may be even more interested in! Maybe we can work this out...." With her good hand, Shauna opened the top two buttons of her long-sleeved shirt, reaching inside to her bra. The soldier that had her gun raised his eyebrows and glanced at his companion. "A trade!" Shauna said quickly, realizing the men may have misunderstood her intent. "Something worth a lot more than a well-used old Glock 19. Look!" She produced one of the gold coins Eric had given her for safekeeping, a half-ounce Krugerrand. There were more of them hidden on her person, including the one-ounce versions wrapped up in the bandage on her hand. "The two of you can split this. It's worth a lot more than it would have been before the crash. The trade value of gold is way more than the cash it would have brought then. Take it!"

"How do we know it's real?" The other soldier asked as Shauna handed it to the one with her gun so he could examine it.

"It's real," the first man said. "I've seen one of these before. She's right, it's worth a lot more than that Glock." He turned back to Shauna. "I won't even ask where you got it, but you've got a deal if you keep it between us." He put the Glock in the envelope and handed it back to her. "Now put this away and don't make me regret this!"

Shauna knew when he agreed to take the gold that these two had no intention of turning in the confiscated weapon. No one would ever know about it but the two of them, because they knew she couldn't go above their heads to complain. They would have kept the Glock to sell or trade, as there was surely a booming black market everywhere, likely even here on the base among the enlisted men. She'd made the right call to offer the coin in trade. The two of them left just as Jonathan returned to the room.

"What was that all about?" Jonathan asked, as Shauna fumbled to rebutton her shirt with one hand.

"They searched our bags. They found the pistol, of course, and they were going to confiscate it, but then I remembered that Eric had given me one of those foreign gold coins of his to hang onto for him; you know, like the ones he used to pay off those guys at the blockade in Florida. It was probably worth more than the Glock, but I knew Eric would want me to have the gun even more, it might be hard to find another one where we're going. I offered the coin to them and they took it! I guess they can hide and get rid of a coin a lot easier than an illegal firearm. I knew we could also get booted off the convoy if it went wrong, but I took a chance."

"So those assholes are just low-life thieves! I thought they were *soldiers!*"

"They are soldiers, but I guess some soldiers are taking advantage of this situation like so many others are. I had no real options. It wasn't like I could report them for trying to steal a gun. We could have been locked up or thrown off the base immediately for having it!"

"No, you did the right thing. That pistol's worth more than any amount of gold, and you're right, we do need it."

Shauna smiled. Jonathan had no idea that she had a lot more gold on her than that one coin, and she had no intention of telling him otherwise unless it was necessary.

Eric had never told him how much there was, and he'd suggested the same to her. It wasn't that Eric didn't trust the kid, it was just that the more people knew, the more potential there was for that knowledge to get them into trouble. Besides, the two of them would be traveling together for an indefinite period now. She figured some other negotiation would eventually arise and Jonathan would find out soon enough. Until then, there was nothing else to say about it.

The two soldiers that had found the gun apparently kept the secret to themselves as promised, and soon Shauna and Jonathan were moving west again on Interstate 70 and finally across the state line into Colorado. Shauna knew Jonathan had never been out of the southeastern United States before this journey, and of course, that explained why his face was glued to the truck window as the landscape changed from cultivated farmlands with ever fewer trees to vast cattle ranches and finally, the expansive vistas of the high plains grasslands. But the scene that really blew him away was the one he stepped out to when the convoy rolled to a stop at a desolate checkpoint near Limon, where it would turn off I-70 to go southwest to Fort Carson.

"Wow! Is that for *real?*" The kid was staring, open-mouthed at the distant blue outline of jagged peaks that dominated the western horizon.

"Yes, it's real all right. They call it the Front Range of the Rockies!" Shauna took a deep breath of the cool, clear air and stared at the rugged mountains with him. She'd seen this view just once before, on the road trip when she and Daniel had driven Megan out to Boulder to get her settled in for her first semester at the university. That seemed so long ago now that Shauna could hardly believe it had only been a little more than two years before. As she looked west to those snowy ramparts again, she knew she was close to her destination and she felt both anticipation and fear in equal measure, not knowing what she would find there. She would have a lot more confidence right now if Eric or even Daniel was here beside her too, but she was grateful she at least had Jonathan, and his enthusiasm for the adventure he perceived in that vista could not be contained.

"That's freaking awesome! I can't wait to get there and see how big they are up close. Are we going to be close to them in Boulder?"

"Oh yeah. A lot closer than we are here, Jonathan, don't worry about that. You're going to see plenty of mountains!"

The last leg of their journey in the company of soldiers was a ride north to the Denver area, arranged the day after the convoy's arrival at Fort Carson. This was a final favor in honor of Lieutenant Holton's request, and Shauna knew they couldn't expect more than that. The driver of the truck dropped them off in the parking lot of an abandoned gas station near the US 36 Bikeway in Westminster and waited while they assembled their bikes.

"The bike path will take you right into the south end of Boulder without having to ride on the highway, although it probably wouldn't make much difference if you did now," he said, looking at the empty roadway.

"Thank you, this is great. We'll find our way from here. I've been to the campus before."

The wide path was like a road itself, well paved and smooth. It would be as easy to ride as any road. When she and Jonathan had checked that the bikes were ready to go, the soldiers drove away, leaving them to finish securing their bags and loading their gear onto the bikes.

"I can't believe how freaking cold it is here, and it's not even winter," Jonathan said, when they finally started riding.

"Winter comes early when you're a mile high, Jonathan. That's why Eric was in a hurry to leave Louisiana. I hope we can find Megan and get out of here before it *really* gets cold, because you haven't seen anything yet. At least it's sunny today and there's no snow and ice on the road to worry about. It could be a lot worse."

"I'm not complaining. It's awesome here, it really is. I'm just not used to cold weather, that's all."

Shauna well understood. She'd been living in south Florida for decades as well, and it was easy to get used to near perpetual summer after all that time. The air was indeed crisp and cold today, especially riding into a light northerly breeze sweeping down the valley. Now that they were on the bikes after hundreds of miles of riding in those Army convoys, she couldn't imagine the hardships of riding all that way on their own power, exposed to the elements all the way. She would have done it, but she was sure glad she didn't have to. Up until the last minute with the soldiers, she had kept hoping that Lieutenant Holton would somehow send word that Eric was back at the post, and that she and Jonathan should wait where they were until he arranged transportation for him to join them, but the finality that it wasn't going to happen hit home when that last truck pulled away, leaving them alone with their bikes.

She was glad it was still early, barely half an hour after noon, because she didn't relish the idea of riding a deserted bike path or city streets in the dark. As it was, there was plenty of time to pedal to the university in the daylight. Seeing all the abandoned businesses here on the outskirts that were closed and shuttered, she fully expected the university and even Megan's apartment complex to be the same, but whether they were or not, she had to go there first in order to start looking. If Megan wasn't there, then perhaps Jonathan was right; and she was safe and warm somewhere in a mountain cabin with friends from the area. That thought was interrupted by a warning from Jonathan:

"Don't look back in an obvious way, but I think we've got company coming."

FERAL NATION: THE DIVIDE

Shauna turned just enough to see in her peripheral vision what Jonathan meant when he said it was on the overpass road they'd just ridden under minutes ago. Four mountain bikes were descending the grassy embankment down to the bike path, and Jonathan whispered that they had turned off the road just seconds after they topped the crest of the overpass and noticed the two of them riding under. Maybe they'd planned to turn there all along, but it seemed odd that they would suddenly make that steep descent when they could have taken the exit earlier. Were they coming after them simply because they wanted to talk to fellow cyclists, or did they see her and Jonathan with their loaded bikes as an unexpected opportunity? She'd seen enough to know that all four riders appeared to be young adult males, and she didn't have a good feeling about being the object of their interest.

Riding close to Jonathan so they could talk in low voices, she shifted gears to get all the speed she could out of the heavy bike. A gradual downhill grade in this stretch of the bikeway made it easier to accelerate, but if those four on their unburdened mountain bikes decided to give chase, they had the advantage of launching a fast pursuit from their steep descent. Shauna reached inside the small bag affixed to her handlebars and felt the reassuring grip of the Glock, running her index finger over the little loaded-chamber indicator button to double-check that she had indeed racked the slide to put a round in the pipe when she inserted a magazine earlier. She hoped she was just being paranoid, but then she heard Jonathan's reaction as he turned and glanced back again.

"Shit! They're still coming; pedaling like hell to catch up!"

Eleven

SHAUNA RISKED ANOTHER QUICK over-the-shoulder glance of her own to confirm what Jonathan told her. The four mountain bikers were gaining on them, pedaling fast in a tight group down the middle of the bike path. Shauna shifted to an even higher gear and stood on her pedals to try and gain more power, thinking that once they were up to speed, the heavier touring bikes she and Jonathan rode might work to their advantage in maintaining momentum downhill. Her injured hand was limiting her ability to accelerate hard though, as she could only use one hand to counter the downward forces of pedaling by pulling up on the bars. Jonathan could probably do better, but he wasn't going to run off and leave her and she knew it. She scanned the pathway ahead as she pedaled, looking for signs of other people who might help them or at least discourage an attack by simply being present to witness, but there was no on to be seen or to see what was about to take place when those four riders caught up with them. It didn't matter that it was the middle of a bright sunny day in what must have once been a safe area for recreational riding, she and Jonathan had attracted the undivided attention of the four determined characters who were now zeroing in to overtake them.

"What do you think, Shauna? Should we just keep pedaling and hope they go on by when they catch up, or should we pull over now and get ready?"

"I don't know yet. I'm thinking! If we let them catch us while we're moving, they could try and cause us to crash. But if we stop, it's going to look like we're expecting or inviting a confrontation. It's a tough call."

"You can't shoot and ride at the same time with only one good hand. Maybe you should give me the pistol."

"If they try something, they'll expect more resistance from you, since you're the guy. It may be better that I'm the one that's armed. That gives me the element of surprise."

Jonathan agreed and said that was good thinking on her part. Shauna hoped he was right, but whether the strategy would work or not depended greatly on whether or not the four overtaking them were also armed. She had to assume they were, but she still wasn't ready to stop until she knew they were going to force it. The small canvas bag the gun was inside was still partially open so she could quickly reach in and grab it, but Jonathan was right, it wouldn't be safe to do that and try to aim too without coming to a stop first. She could steer with her injured hand but putting all her weight on it to steady the bike enough for shooting was a different matter altogether. And the riders behind them were closing to inside of a hundred feet by now, a couple of them already shouting "Hey!" and "Wait up, what's your hurry?"

"I hope we can talk our way out of this, Jonathan, but I'm not counting on it."

"I'll bet they think we have all kinds of good stuff in these bags. Maybe we can make them think we'll give it to them without a fight."

"Well, we can't outrun them, that's for sure, but let's see what they do when they get closer. If it's clear that they are going to try something, then you yell and hit your brakes hard and make them think you're stopping to protect me. That might give me enough time to create some distance and get into position to shoot if I have to."

Shauna glanced back again and saw that whatever was going to happen, it was imminent. The four riders had spread apart across the 12-foot width of the bike path, running abreast of each other as they pedaled from the standing position. When the one nearest her saw her look back, he shouted again: "Hey baby! You're new in town, aren't you? Hold up! We just want to talk!"

Shauna ignored him and pedaled harder. Jonathan was still beside her for now and they exchanged glances, each of them knowing this was indeed going to be trouble. Another of the riders commented on the shape of her rear end and made a derogatory remark about the 'punk' accompanying her. Two of them were almost on her back wheel now and when she glanced over her shoulder, she saw they were about Jonathan's age themselves but had the manner of street thugs who certainly weren't new to the lifestyle in just the short period since the fall of law and order. When she looked across to Jonathan's other side, she saw that the rider pulling alongside him had a three-foot stick that appeared to be a cut-down pool cue in one hand. Just when she thought he was going to take a swing at the kid's head and was hoping Jonathan would stop suddenly as agreed, the attacker instead shoved the stick into his rear spokes, causing the wheel to instantly lock up, slamming him and the bike to the hard asphalt.

Shauna screamed Jonathan's name as all four of the riders howled with laughter. She saw the kid roll to his hands and knees as his tumble came to an end and wondered if he'd broken any bones. Regardless, he couldn't help her now and her best hope was to appear terrified and helpless, if only long enough to get her hand on that Glock. She braked to a stop before she was knocked down as well, pleading with them not to hurt Jonathan as they began jumping off their bikes to follow up their attack. "Please! Just leave us alone! We don't have anything you want! We're just trying to get home!"

The biggest of the four, wild-eyed, wiry and covered in tats to the top of his neck, kicked Jonathan hard in the stomach before he could get to his feet, and then looked Shauna up and down. "Oh, I think you do! I think you need to party with us for a while!"

"You can have our money!" Shauna said, reaching into the handlebar bag. "There's a lot of cash in here! It's all we have left but take it! Please! Just let us be on our way!"

His eyes followed her hand to the bag, interested, but then he was distracted by the sound of Jonathan gasping for breath after the vicious kick, still down and unable to get up. One of the other gang members pulled something from his jeans pocket and Shauna heard the loud metallic click as the blade of a six-inch folder snapped open in his hand. He took a step towards the kid, brandishing the menacing blade.

"DO IT!" The big one ordered.

Shauna knew then it was now or never. This man had just ordered his buddy to finish Jonathan. She would be next whenever they were done with her, that was inevitable. She might not be able to get them all before they got to her, but she knew she had to try. Eric's patient instruction and hours of working with her, drilling the reflexes and focusing on the front sight replayed in her mind despite the years that intervened as she drew the Glock in one smooth motion and brought it into line with the knife wielder's torso. A face shot would be better, as Eric always said, but the man was already bent over and turned to one side, having grabbed Jonathan by the hair to pull his head back and expose his throat. All four of the thugs were momentarily distracted by the spectacle, and that was their fatal mistake, giving her the split-second window that Shauna needed to aim and fire. She squeezed off a rapid double tap into the ribs of that guy and then moved her front sight in line with the big, tatted one as he spun around at the sound of the gunfire with a stunned look on his face. Shauna didn't miss. He was less than ten feet away and this time she did aim for the face, needing only one round to ensure that she was the last thing that sorry excuse for a human ever saw. One of the remaining two was scrambling to grab his bike and get on it, but the last one was fumbling with something at his waistband. Shauna shot him twice as he tried to rack the slide to chamber a round in the little chrome-plated semi-auto he produced. As he fell, she put her sight squarely on the back of the last one, who was now up on the pedals, desperately trying to leave the scene. It would have been an easy shot, but Shauna couldn't do it. The punk was no longer a threat and she doubted he would even think about coming back. She turned to Jonathan, who was getting his breath back while staring at her in wide-eyed amazement.

"Damn! That was some awesome shooting, Shauna! I knew Eric taught you how to handle guns, but wow! I had no idea you were that good! That was like John Wick shit!"

"It wasn't anything special, Jonathan, just the element of surprise, like we talked about. Are you okay?"

Jonathan got to his feet before she could give him a hand. She saw that his hands and elbows were bleeding from where he'd skidded on the pavement. It looked painful, but he shrugged it off. "Nothing's broken, just a little road rash, that's all. You saved my life, though! Thank you! That guy was going to freakin' cut my throat!"

"And mine too, I'm sure. They made the mistake of thinking I was easy pickings after they knocked you down. Thank God and Lieutenant Holton for this Glock, or we'd both be dead!" Shauna looked around, checking to make sure the bike path was still deserted. She'd just killed three men in broad daylight and didn't know for certain that no one had witnessed it. But looking around now, it appeared they were alone. The one guy she'd let get away had turned off the path at the first opportunity and disappeared. She doubted he would go looking for the authorities if there were even any to be found nearby, but now that the shooting was over, she was shaken by the encounter and even more frightened for Megan. It didn't bode well for what they would find at the university that something like this had happened so shortly after their arrival. Shauna ejected the partially-empty magazine from her pistol and slammed home a fresh one with the full 15 rounds. After this encounter, the paltry six mags that Lieutenant Holton had given her didn't seem adequate at all, and she understood why Eric had insisted on carrying so much firepower when they first left Bart's place.

Jonathan had already picked up the small pistol that the third guy had drawn.

"Lorcin L380 is what it says on here," he said, reading the markings on the slide. "It's a .380 caliber. That's pretty small, isn't it? It looks like it only holds seven rounds."

"See if he's got another magazine on him. It's not much of a weapon, but it might be better than nothing next time something like this happens. I'll check these other guys too."

"Can you still ride?" She asked Jonathan, after finding no other weapons on them other than the big Cold Steel folder that she put in her bag with her magazines.

"I think so but look at my bike! That back wheel is trashed!"

Shauna knew this already. The bike was still laying in the road where it had slid to a stop. The stick going into the spokes at speed had broken nearly half of them before locking up the wheel. As a consequence, the rim was bent and twisted beyond repair. "What about their bikes? Will one of their back wheels fit yours?"

"That one will," he said, nodding at the one the guy wielding the stick had been riding. "It's got 26-inch wheels. Those other two look like 29er's to me. I could ride one those, but I like the way this Specialized is set up and I've already got my loading system figured out. I'll swap the wheel, but I think I'm going to have to straighten out the derailleur too. It's a wonder I didn't break my neck after that bastard took me down like that. He got what he deserved, that's for sure."

Shauna knew Jonathan was right about that last, but she was a little pale now after searching the bodies of the three young men, none of them much older than Jonathan or her own Megan. The bandage on her hand was a vivid reminder that this wasn't her first gunfight since this surreal situation began, but this encounter was up close and personal. There'd been no other choice though and that she had to do it, or she and Jonathan would be the ones left there in the bike path. But the knowledge that she was right still didn't make her feel particularly good about taking three lives. She wanted to get away from this scene and put it behind her now, so she did what she could to help Jonathan get his bike rolling again. The borrowed wheel worked, and after some adjustments, to the brakes and derailleur, Jonathan was ready to ride again.

"Should we try to drag them off the path?" Jonathan asked, as Shauna was already mounting her bike and preparing to ride.

"No. Let's get out of here before more of their friends or the police come along." Shauna considered trying to take a different route into Boulder, but the highway that paralleled this bike path was just as visible if not more so to anyone who might still be at home in the adjacent neighborhoods they had to pass.

Sure enough, they had only gone a quarter of a mile after leaving the scene of the shooting when just such a neighborhood appeared on the left. Shauna glanced over at the nearest house and saw a middle-aged man staring at them where he stood in his yard behind a board fence. She wondered if he had heard the gunfire and was staring now to memorize their descriptions, so he could report them to the authorities, but he gave her a friendly wave when he realized she'd seen him, so maybe not. Shauna pretended to ignore him, keeping her head down so that her face was less visible until they were well out of sight.

"I wonder how many more people might be around in these houses that we can't see?" Jonathan said.

"Probably not many, but you never know. I don't like this though. It's creeping me out, knowing we're probably being watched and that we might run into another gang like that first one."

"Yeah, me too, but what can we do about it? Just keep riding, I guess."

"That's all."

An hour after the attack, they passed a sign indicating they were in the city limits of Boulder and then another indicating the direction to the university. Thankfully, they were in a long, straight stretch of the route and could see a good distance ahead as they neared the campus.

"That looks like a checkpoint," Jonathan said, slowing and then stopping in front of Shauna.

She pulled up beside him and they tried to discern what they were seeing; whether it was the military, or perhaps police or something else. "We'd better find a place to hide these guns before we ride any closer."

"You want to go up there?"

"Of course. That's the campus dead ahead. That's what we came all this way for."

"We'll be screwed if some thief finds your Glock before we come back for it."

"Then let's find a really good place to hide it so that won't happen."

They turned around and rode far enough back to be hidden from view of anyone manning the checkpoint who might be watching through binoculars and then turned off into a small wooded park, where they found loose rocks beneath which to conceal the handguns and magazines. She was quite sure they weren't being watched, but she stretched and walked around like she was just out for her daily exercise, trying to draw the attention of any unseen prying eyes to herself while Jonathan quickly and discreetly tucked the weapons out of sight. Then, they remounted their bikes and rode in the direction of the manned barricades they'd seen in the distance.

Unlike the bigger Army checkpoints they'd seen while in the supply convoy on the highways, this one appeared to be manned by civilian forces and it didn't appear busy, as there was virtually no traffic on the road even here in town. Shauna felt her stomach twist into knots as she wondered whether they'd be allowed to pass and whether Megan was just over there, beyond that barricade on the other side. Anything could happen when approaching the authorities like this, and even though they'd ditched their firearms they could be arrested simply for being here, but Shauna was determined to explain her purpose and tell the truth to the extent it was required. The two of them pedaled until they were within hailing distance of the men manning the roadblock, and then they got off to walk their bikes the rest of the forward to the parked vehicles and barricades that blocked the road ahead.

"There's no access at this checkpoint," one of the guards said when Shauna said they were trying to enter the campus. "If you're seeking refuge, you'll have to go to the main gateway. Turn back one block and go east on that road until you come to the second intersection. Turn left there and follow that road until you see a building directly ahead with posted guards outside. If you can show I.D. to prove you're local, they may be able to process you today."

"We're not looking for refuge," Shauna said. "I have to find my daughter. She's a student at the university and lives near the campus." Shauna named the apartment complex.

151

"The university is closed indefinitely and has been for months," the guard said. "Most of the campus facilities have been converted in a refugee center for the students as well as local civilians. If your daughter was a student there, chances are, she's either among the refugees or detainees."

"Detainees?"

"Troublemakers. The category into which a whole lot of former students fell into, I'm afraid. Those arrested for rioting, looting and other crimes. If your daughter is among that group, she'll be there until order is restored and trials can be held."

Shauna was lost in thought for a moment. This was something she'd feared all along when she hadn't heard from Megan even before the hurricane in Florida made it impossible for her to call. "How do I find out if she's there?"

"I'm don't know if you can. All I can tell you to do is go to the processing center and ask someone there. They may be able to help you, but we can't here. My job is to prevent access, and I'm going to ask you two to move along."

"Wow, the freaking campus is a refugee center now? That sounds like some of the places I heard they were setting up around Orlando and Tampa before I met Eric," Jonathan said, as the two of them turned back to follow the route the guard had given them.

"They better not be holding my Megan with those detainees," Shauna said. "I know she wouldn't have been involved in violent rioting. At least not willingly."

"We won't know until we get there. I guess they'll ask us a bunch of questions, especially when they find out we're both from Florida. Do you think they'll believe our crazy story about how we got here? What if they lock us up too?"

"I don't know what they'll believe or what they'll say Jonathan, but I'm not leaving until I find out about Megan, I can tell you that, no matter what I have to do. You can wait back at that park if you'd rather. There's no need for you to go there with me."

"Oh hell no. I'm going. I didn't come all this way for nothing. It's just too bad you had to give that gold coin of Eric's to those asshole soldiers back in Kansas. Something like that would probably get us in the door, or at least get us some answers. Now, we don't have anything of value worth to bribe anybody with."

Shauna said nothing, but Jonathan had a point. If she could get to one person who could make a decision, the right offer might buy either access or answers. At this point, it might be all she had left to try. Jonathan didn't have a clue about the gold she was still carrying, but it was something to think about. She thought about the questions she would ask as they pedaled, until finally they made the last turn and saw the building the guard had told them about.

Twelve

SHAUNA FOUND THE PROCESSING office of the refugee center easier to approach than she'd expected. The reason, of course, was that there weren't any actual refugees wanting to get in at the moment, as most people in the immediate area were either already there or had left for other parts. Most of those inside were city and suburban folks with no safe place to go and no way to survive with the crippled infrastructure and lack of services and basic necessities. The female officer named Tonya that she and Jonathan found themselves talking to informed them that the refugee camp offered safety, protection from the elements, and food, which was something most of those on the outside didn't have unless they were far more self-sufficient and prepared than the average citizen.

The processing center did have an offline computer database with information on those inside, however, and after Shauna managed to convince the woman that she was indeed who she said she was, Tonya pulled up the list and searched for Megan, but came up with nothing.

"She's not here."

"Are you sure? Maybe she didn't get entered into the system."

"No, if she was inside, there would be a record on her, whether she was in the free refugee section or among the detainees," Tonya said, with a tone of finality that suggested there were no further options.

"Maybe she was here and left? Maybe she decided to go someplace else, or even try to make it home somehow?"

"No, that's impossible. If she was ever here at all, it would be in here. If someone leaves, dies or their status changes in any way, we have to update it."

"And you're sure you have *everybody*? I mean, she was a student on the university and living in an apartment right by the campus before all this was established. Wouldn't there be a chance that some of the students who were already here just stayed and didn't get entered into the system?"

"The entire campus was under lockdown and there was a room to room search in every building after the riots, including all the apartment complexes. It was absolutely secured, believe me. They had to do a clean sweep to get the situation back under control."

"What was the reason for the riots? What happened?" Jonathan asked.

"Who can list all the reasons? It started with protests that became violent. The police intervened of course, and people got hurt. Others were killed as the situation escalated; police, students and other non-participants caught up in it."

Shauna felt a wave of panic upon hearing this. Tonya could see what she was thinking.

"I already scanned the list of the deceased as we were talking. Megan Branson's name doesn't show up there either. All I can tell you is that she's not here and never was."

"What about her roommate? Can you check that for me? Her name is Vicky Singleton? Is she in your database?"

Shauna looked at Jonathan while they waited for the new search to complete. When Tonya said Vicky's name didn't show up either, Shauna felt the knots twisting tighter.

"You said she might have a boyfriend out here," Jonathan said.

"I don't know if he was a *boyfriend*, but she mentioned this Gareth guy a few times during her first semester. I don't remember if she ever told me his last name though. There was another girlfriend she talked about a lot though." Shauna turned back to Tonya. "Can you try the name, Jena Anderson? I think she lived in the apartment next door to Megan and Nikki."

"Ah yes. Got it! I do have a Jena Adams, age 19, in the system. It shows she is in the detention section, charged with rioting. Not surprising, really. Like I said, there were a lot of them. Mostly university students, but a few faculty members as well."

"I've got to talk to her!" Shauna said. "Jena may know why Megan and Vicky aren't here. Maybe she knows where they went."

"I'm sorry, but I'm afraid that's not allowed. Unless you're a family member or her attorney, you can't visit with a detainee in lockup."

This was the answer Shauna was afraid she would hear as soon as she learned that Jena was indeed in that section of the refugee center. Shauna didn't know anything about this girl, other than that Megan had said she was cool and that they were hanging out a lot. She *had* to speak with her though because right now she was the only connection to her daughter that Shauna could think of. Looking at Jonathan and then back at Tonya, Shauna realized the one thing she had to her advantage was that the three of them were alone together in Tonya's office. This woman alone was *the* deciding factor on whether or not Shauna got to see Jena.

"Please! Just give me ten minutes with her. Can't you put down that I *am* family? Her aunt maybe? Who will know the difference? It's your decision, right?"

"Yes, it is, and my job is to make sure everyone entering this facility is properly identified and vetted. If your daughter was inside, I could get you in. If you were from Boulder County, I could get you in through refugee status. As it is, you're neither local nor immediate family to anyone inside who is."

"I understand your job must be tough," Shauna said. "I understand that just living here must have its share of hardships with no immediate end in sight. Do you have a family? Children of your own?"

Tonya looked back at Shauna, hesitating at first, before saying that she did. "We are all doing the best we can here."

"Wouldn't this help you out? Something with which to barter for some extra little luxuries, maybe?" Shauna slid a half-Krugerrand across the desk, leaving it in front of her. "This is a half-ounce of gold. It's a lot better than cash. I only need a few minutes. Five or ten at the most. You can tell the guards that I'm Jena's aunt and that we're passing through and just wanted to check on her and make sure she was okay."

"I could end up in there myself if this got out," Tonya said.

"It won't. I won't say anything to anyone. I just want to see if Jena knows where Megan went."

Tonya picked up the coin, turning it in her fingers to look at both sides. "Is it really worth so much to you just to talk to a girl who may not have the answers you want?"

"Wouldn't it be to you, if your daughter was the one missing? That gold is just a means to an end, like any other form of currency. My husband brought it when he returned to the United States because he knew we'd probably need it. So yes, it's absolutely worth it to me, and I know you can put it to good use buying things you need for your family. Do we have a deal?"

"It's too risky to try to get him in too," she said, nodding at Jonathan. "You'll have to go alone. It'll raise fewer questions that way."

"That's fine. If Jonathan can wait here for me. I'm sure he won't mind."

"Yeah, I'm totally good with it," Jonathan said. "I don't really want to go inside a place like this anyway. Fences and guards and stuff creep me out. It feels too much like a prison to me. You go. I'll be waiting when you get back."

While she waited for Tonya to make the necessary call, Shauna asked to use the restroom and while inside she quickly removed her socks and the remaining gold coins hidden on her person, putting the coins into one of them and passing it off to Jonathan when Tonya wasn't watching. She assumed she would be thoroughly searched for weapons and contraband before she was admitted through the gates, and she couldn't afford to lose the last of her bargaining power. Jonathan gave her a surprised but knowing look when he felt the weight of the sock before slipping it into a pocket. Once she was inside, Shauna was met by a security officer from the detainment sector, and he drove her to the building used for that purpose in an open-topped Jeep Wrangler. Along the short drive, Shauna saw very few of the 'free' inhabitants of the converted campus, and when she asked the guard where everybody was, he just said most of them spent their time indoors. Shauna couldn't imagine what it was like for those who had no other choice but to seek out a place like this in order to survive, but she knew she and Daniel and Andrew would have been facing the same fate in Florida if not for Bart's place on the Caloosahatchee River. She was certain that the 'detainment sector' of this place would be far bleaker, but the guard told her that the ones being held here weren't the worst offenders. Those were in another facility off-site. Tonya hadn't mentioned that, and now Shauna had something else to worry about. Could Megan possibly be there instead? She put the thought out of her mind for now. First, she had to talk to Jena. When they arrived and went inside the converted building, Shauna was taken to a small office near the front where a guard stood watch outside the door. Through the glass, Shauna saw a young woman seated inside and she easily recognized her from the pictures Megan had texted months before. She was allowed inside alone with her, while her escort waited outside with the other guard.

"Jena Adams? I'm Shauna Hartfield. Megan Branson's mom."

"Really? You're Megan's mom? Oh wow, I thought you lived like way far away. Florida, right?"

"Yes, I did, but I've been trying to reach Megan since before the beginning of summer. I haven't talked to her at all since the cell networks went down. Please tell me you know where she is, Jena! When is the last time you saw her?"

Jena looked back at her, lost in thought as if she were trying to remember. "It wasn't long before they put me in here. A week maybe? I don't know, everything was crazy on campus for a while. It was just one big riot, day and night. I didn't want to leave, because I thought it would stop, but Megan said she wasn't staying."

"Where was she going? Did she say? She didn't leave alone did she?"

"No, she was with Gareth, and her roommate, Nikki. There were some other people with them too. They were going to get the hell out of here and go to some ranch way out in the mountains. It's where Nikki's grandparents live. She said it would be safe there, and Gareth said it would be better to get out of the cities and towns too, so that's what they did. They asked me to go with them, but Toby wouldn't do it, and I wasn't about to leave him. He was so awesome!"

Shauna noticed tears forming in Jena's eyes.

"He's your boyfriend?"

"He *was*," she said, staring off into space as if lost for a moment. "But he's dead now. He got shot by those soldiers they sent here. A lot of people did, and then the rest of us were arrested. They brought us here later after they turned our campus into a prison!" She glared at the two guards outside the door.

Shauna didn't know what to say. It was a huge relief to know that Megan had left before all that happened, but that didn't mean she was safe. Shauna had to find out where that ranch was, and then get there with Jonathan as soon as possible.

"They were going to hike there," Jena said, when Shauna asked her how they planned to reach the ranch. "Gareth knows the mountains around here better than any of our friends. He said there were trails that were shortcuts and that it would be a lot safer than being on the roads. He knows what he's doing. I'm sure they made it just fine," Jena said, but it's been a long time now. I can't see Gareth just hanging out at some ranch, doing nothing, with all that's going on everywhere."

"What do mean? I thought you just said he wanted to go there because it was away from everything."

"He did, I think. But Gareth isn't the type to just hide out and not get involved. He wants to help people. He saw that it wasn't going to work to stay here and fight, but that doesn't mean he's given up the fight."

Shauna considered this for a minute, trying to understand. *Was this Gareth some kind of activist who'd been in the middle of the trouble that landed Jena in here and got her boyfriend killed? Was Megan involved in it too?* She wasn't sure if she wanted to know the answer to that right now, but she definitely wanted directions to that ranch. Jena had never been there, of course, but she knew some of the nearby mountain towns and she knew the name of the valley where the ranch was located, as well as the name of the ranch itself.

"Nikki's grandparents have lived there like forever, I think. She said they have horses there. It's pretty far from any main roads. I think it's just a gravel road for a long way before you get there, but it's close to the Continental Divide Trail, and that's the way Gareth planned to go."

The guards opening the door was their sign that Shauna's brief visitation time was up. It was just as well. She had about all the information that Jena could give her. As she rode back to the front gate with the security officer, she wondered what the odds were that Megan was still at that ranch, if she had gotten there at all. There were still as many questions as answers, but at least she had something—a new goal to reach that might or might not be the end of her search. Jonathan was going to see his mountains all right—the very heart of the Rockies as they crossed the Continental Divide. When she was taken back to Tonya's office, he jumped up from the chair, wanting to know what she'd learned from Jena, but she put him off for a moment, whispering for him to give her the sock and give her a few more minutes while he waited outside.

"Thank you so much for what you did. It means the world to me," Shauna told Tonya when Jonathan left. "At least I know where to start looking, but I have one more favor to ask before I go."

"I don't think there's anything else I can do to help you today. You should probably just leave now while you're ahead."

"It's not much. All I need is a piece of paper and an envelope. I need to leave a message with you in case someone else shows up here looking for my daughter. It's a slim chance, but it's possible her father will find his way here later if he's still alive. He would have no idea where to go other than here to the campus, and he doesn't even know the names of Megan's friends like I did."

"There's no guarantee that I'll even be assigned here when and if he comes. You can leave the letter, I suppose, but don't expect me to actually get it to him. It's unlikely to happen."

"I understand, but if you can try, I would really appreciate it, and it will be worth your while. Shauna put another half-Krugerrand coin in Tonya's hand, surely incentive enough for her to pay attention to anyone who might come here inquiring about Megan Branson. It was a lot to give her, but Shauna's brief visit with Jena had been more than worth it already. "Eric, my husband, has more of those, and I'm sure he'll be happy to reward you as well for giving him the letter after you tell him that Jonathan and I were here."

Tonya put the coin away quickly and gave Shauna the pen and paper she requested. When Shauna finished and sealed the brief one-page letter in the envelope, she handed it over and thanked the woman again.

"I will do my best to watch for your husband. Good luck to you."

Shauna left the office and found Jonathan waiting outside the door.

"Are you gonna tell me what you found out now?"

"Yes. Let's just get on our bikes and ride back to that park. We'll talk on our way there. We've got another journey ahead of us, Jonathan, and it's going to take us *that way*." Shauna pointed west, to the rugged peaks rising up against the skyline. By the time they'd retrieved the Glock and its magazines, along with the junk pistol taken off the dead gang member, she had told the kid everything she knew.

"So, this Gareth dude, her boyfriend I guess, figured out they'd better get out of town before they got arrested?"

"I don't know if he's actually a *boyfriend*. If he was, Jena didn't say."

"Even if he wasn't back then, they might have hooked up once all the riots started. Sounds like that dude was a troublemaker to me."

"Maybe, but maybe not. At least he seemed to have enough sense to get out of here while they still could. If they were going to a remote ranch, there's probably not a lot of trouble they could get into out there. I think the *real* troublemakers stuck around the cities and college campuses because that's where the action was. I don't think Megan would get involved in any of that, certainly not the violence. I know her well enough to know that she would never intentionally hurt someone unless it was self-defense."

"So how are we supposed to get to this place? Is it like a real deal cowboy ranch with horses and stuff?"

"I don't know, but probably. This is ranch country out here, Jonathan, at least outside of the urban areas."

"Do you know how far away it is?"

"Not exactly. I know they were planning on hiking there on a series of trails that would keep them off the roads, including The Continental Divide Trail. Jena told me that if we head west on Highway 119 we will come to where it crosses. If we follow it south it's a shortcut to the valley where the ranch is. We'll have to turn off on a gravel forest service road that the trail intersects and follow it west. That's about all she could tell me, that and the name of Vicky's grandparents that are the owners of the ranch."

"Can we ride our bikes down that trail?"

"I don't think so. Jena said it's a hiking trail. That usually means steep and difficult going even on foot. We can ride *to* it though. Or we can try and find our way to the road the long way around, but Jena said it's much farther because there's no pass for a road unless you go way to the south first and then double back."

"I say we hike it then. I'm up for it if you are."

"I'm up for whatever it takes. You should know that by now, but I might be hesitant to try and hike a trail like that all alone, so I'm glad you're going too. I don't think it'll be easy, but after what happened today on the road, I think I'd rather be out in the wilderness, wouldn't you? If we can get out of town without running into more trouble, we'll probably be fine in the mountains."

"Unless we run into a freakin' bear or mountain lion," Jonathan said.

"Don't let that worry you. Animals aren't nearly as likely to bother us as people are. I'll take my chances with them any day. The main thing we need to worry about up there is the weather. The sooner we get to that ranch, the better, because every day that passes, gets us closer to winter, and like I said before, winter comes early out here. You don't want to be caught in the high country in a snowstorm."

Thirteen

ERIC AND SERGEANT CONNELLY were locked up alone together in a shared cell, but several other prisoners in Sheriff Morgan's jail were close enough to converse with, and the two of them learned that most of their fellow inmates were in there for minor infractions rather than real crimes.

"Nobody gets a trial anymore, and there's no bail or nothing. The sheriff decides what the sentence is, and there's only two ways out of here: Either he figures you've done your time and he gives you a second chance, or it straight out back to the hangman's noose."

Eric wasn't sure if the man was yanking his chain or being serious, but he didn't dismiss the latter possibility either. "You've seen this?" he asked.

"Everybody around here has. It's been going on since about the middle of summer when all the trouble started. Most people they lock up aren't in here but a couple of days if they're in for a hanging offense. The rest of us are just waiting for our time to be up, but as far as I know, the only ones that have been let loose are local folks, like me.

Strangers usually don't get a second chance. I don't think your prospects are looking too good, if you get my drift."

Eric did, but he wasn't going to let it get to him. He knew that's what this guy was trying to do, but despite the fact they'd been arrested on the spot, Sheriff Morgan seemed like a somewhat reasonable man to him. Like he'd jokingly mentioned to his own brother Keith when he still had his personal M4, he knew that unlicensed possession of a fully automatic rifle was a felony back in normal times. And he knew too that in many areas, especially around the bigger cities, possession of any firearm could get you shot. But he had to believe that out here in a place like this, where most folks owned and carried guns even before, it would be considered foolish to go around without one now. He hoped too that Sheriff Morgan would give some thought to what Sergeant Connelly had told him and at least try to verify their story. Whether he would or not and how long it might take him to do so was anybody's guess. In the meantime, they were simply stuck. It gave him and Sergeant Connelly lots of time to get to know each other though, swapping war stories and recounting their experiences here in the States since the breakdown began.

"After seeing what my brother, Keith has been dealing with since this happened, I can understand the need for law enforcement to take a hardline approach," Eric said, as he told Sergeant Connelly what he'd seen in south Louisiana.

"Most of his department was wiped out, including the sheriff."

"We've heard the rumors about the Gulf Coast. You're the only one I've gotten a first-hand report from down there though, and certainly the first I've talked to that's seen the aftermath of that storm in south Florida. You've been through hell since the day you came ashore, haven't you? I feel even worse than I did before about you risking everything all over again to get me out. Now you've gotten yourself into a situation there may not be a way out of."

"There's always a way out," Eric said. "We just bide our time and see what happens. I may be wrong, but I don't think we're in line for the gallows just yet. But while we're here with nothing else to do but talk to pass the time, I'd want to know everything you can think of that might help me when I head out West."

"I wish I could share your optimism that you'll get to make that trip, and I suppose I should, considering what you've accomplished so far. It's just that I have my doubts about Sheriff Morgan bothering himself to make a radio call."

"Well, he can't keep us in here indefinitely. He doesn't have room for that, so either he lets us go or he does away with us. If he picks the second option, there's nothing else to plan for. But if I get out of here, I'm getting you back to your post and then I'll be carrying on to Boulder. I hope Shauna and Jonathan are still waiting on me, but if they aren't, it's because they're already on their way there."

"So, you really think she and that Florida kid will go on without you, huh?"

"I know Shauna will, and Jonathan hasn't got anything better to do, so he'll go with her. Lieutenant Holton damned sure better honor his word to help them, though. I'd hate to think about just the two of them trying to ride all that way alone."

"Knowing the lieutenant like I do, I'd say he will. He's not one to go back on his word, even if he doesn't always make the best decisions. He's gotta cover his ass doing something as unorthodox as sending a civilian on a recon mission like the one you just did for him though. You know how it works."

Eric did, and he was over being pissed off about it. What was done, was done, and the real problem now was getting out of this shithole jail in the middle of nowhere. But it was getting harder to think about that or anything else while he was locked in there with the sergeant because their new friends in the neighboring cells wouldn't shut up with their questions and their dire predictions of the fate that surely awaited them here. Days of this dragged by until they turned into a week and then two. Then one morning shortly after sunrise, when Sheriff Morgan himself, accompanied by two deputies came to open their cell door, the other inmates burst into a frenzy.

"I told you what was going to happen," the most vocal of them said. "You're going swinging this morning! Isn't that right, Sheriff Morgan? You're still stretching in that new rope, aren't you?"

"You might get your chance to help me with that yourself, Hollis, if you don't mind your own business," Sheriff Morgan said, as he slammed the door shut on the empty cell and led Eric and Sergeant Connelly out to the main door.

Eric smiled at that but said nothing. He didn't get the feeling they were being marched to the gallows, especially since they weren't even put in handcuffs when they were let out of their cell. He saw that he was right when they continued around the block to the courthouse, where they were taken inside to the sheriff's office.

"Well, I guess it turns out you boys weren't lying were, you? No matter how much of a tall tale it seemed like y'all were telling."

"You used the radio frequencies I gave you?" Sergeant Connelly asked. "It sure took you long enough to get through. Did you speak to Lieutenant Holton?"

"Yes sir, I did, Sergeant Connelly. He was mighty surprised to find out you were still alive, you and your Navy SEAL buddy both. You see it turns out that another game warden from the neighboring county saw a military-looking patrol boat come up the river just a couple days after we brought you boys in. He didn't know the story here at the time and didn't think too much about it. Then he ran into one of the guys from my county—one of the fellows who was with us that day—and when they got to talking, the subject came up. When our warden came and told me, I drove up there and got the one that saw the boat to give me the details of it, and it sounded just like the one you described that you said those terrorists down at the lake stole from you. He said it had a machine gun and everything, and that the crew looked like Army or Marines or something, he wasn't sure. They didn't see him because he wasn't in his boat. He was watching the river from up on a bluff that day and not knowing what those fellows were up to, he stayed out of sight. Once I had that information, I decided I'd better try those frequencies and see if they amounted to anything. The radio operator there finally put that lieutenant on and when I described you fellows to him he about blew up. He's sending a helicopter down here this morning to pick y'all up."

Eric felt like punching the dumbass sheriff, but nothing he could say or do would bring back those lost days—days that by now would have seen him in Colorado, possibly already reunited with Megan. The prospect of a helicopter ride back to the post was great, but would Shauna and Jonathan still be there when he arrived?

"I do apologize for any inconvenience your stay in my little county hotel might have caused. You've got to understand though, in the situation we're in, I've got to keep a close eye on that river and the roads that run through my jurisdiction. I can't begin to tell you about all the trouble we've had here since this damned country started blowing up all around us. I know you fellows are the good guys now, the ones trying to do something about it, and applaud your efforts, I really do. I'm sorry about the men you lost down there too, Sergeant Connelly."

Sheriff Morgan returned their confiscated belongings, including the M4 and the Beretta and the remaining hand grenades that were in Eric's bags. Eric had no further use for the compound bow nor the boat, outboard and gasoline he'd paid dearly for, so there was nothing to do but leave them. A helicopter ride back to the post was worth far more than the alternative. When the bird arrived and landed in an empty parking lot across from the courthouse at 0930, Eric saw that it was a UH-72 Lakota, and he naturally thought it was the same one aboard which he flew to the lake that night. He realized his mistake when he saw the unfamiliar flight crew, however, and he and Sergeant Connelly both were a little let down that they didn't get a chance to have a word with the pilot that turned tail and ran at the first sign of hostile fire from the lake that night.

When Lieutenant Holton met them upon their arrival at the post, Eric learned immediately that Shauna and Jonathan had left nearly ten days prior, just as he'd feared would happen while he was sitting in jail all that time. Before he could get all the details about that though, he had to sit through a debriefing with Lieutenant Holton and Sergeant Connelly, retelling the sequence of events from the time he left that helicopter until he and the sergeant were arrested. When that was finally done, Sergeant Connelly was taken away to get medical attention for his knee, leaving Eric alone with the lieutenant to iron out what was going to happen next.

"I know they arrived in a place called Westminster, between Denver and Boulder. They were dropped off by a truck from Fort Carson. They had two of the three bicycles that you had with you on the towboat, and I made sure they were supplied with all the MREs they could carry."

"What about weapons? Please tell me they weren't dumped out there unarmed."

"Of course not, Branson. I supplied your wife with a Glock 19 and plenty of mags. I would have given her a rifle too, but she couldn't have hidden it. I'm sure the two of them are just fine. From what I was told they would only have to ride a short distance on a bike path to reach that campus, and from word I got back from Fort Carson, the city of Boulder is locked down tight by local security forces. I'll bet they're with your daughter already, and that all three of them are just fine."

"I've got to get there yesterday!" Eric said. "After all I've done for you, Lieutenant, I expect to find my ass on a plane or helicopter, ASAP!"

"I anticipated that Branson, and I've been working on arrangements all morning. You'll be in Boulder before this time tomorrow. As soon as it's refueled, the UH-72 that brought you and Connelly back will take you north to the Air Guard base in Springfield. There's a C130 leaving this afternoon for another Air Guard base in Cheyenne. From there, you'll get a helicopter ride to Boulder first thing in the morning. They'll set you down at a checkpoint as close to that campus as possible, and someone there will drive you the rest of the way in. After your wife and nephew left here, I wasn't in direct communication with the various units they were traveling with. I didn't know that last truck driver was going to drop them off as far from the campus as he did. They had their bikes though, so I'm sure it didn't take them long to get there. Given the situation, I think it turned out as good as anyone could hope for, but you'll get there even faster."

"I appreciate it, Lieutenant Holton. I'm going to need some gear though—weapons, food, and a rucksack—I'd rather travel light and not bother with the bike since I'll have a ride all the way to the campus. I'll just leave it here if you don't mind."

"Suit yourself. We'll find someone who can use it, and I don't blame you, I wouldn't want to be out on the roads on a bicycle these days either, I'll tell you that. I don't think you'll have to worry that your wife will be either. From the little I talked to her, she seems pretty level-headed. If she found your daughter there at that refugee center, I'll bet they'll settle in for a while. She hadn't given up on you when she left here either, she just knew it didn't make sense to stay here waiting. She'll do her waiting out there instead, if I had to guess."

Eric knew that whatever the lieutenant might think she'd do, he didn't know Shauna. She *was* level-headed, at least most of the time, but she wouldn't sit around and wait anywhere for long unless she knew it was the best option available to her. If she did find Megan at that refugee center, she was going to do everything in her power to convince her that they needed to get to Keith's if at all possible. Shauna would know there was strength in family sticking together, and besides, she wouldn't want to leave Keith and Bart hanging any longer than necessary, much less Daniel and Andrew. Lieutenant Holton had told her Eric was missing in action, and as likely dead as not. Eric didn't think she would give Megan false hope that her dad was on his way and sit there hoping. She would tell her the truth; that they both had to assume he wasn't coming unless proven otherwise. That's why Eric had to get there fast. Maybe, just maybe, it wasn't too late to intercept them before they were lost on the road somewhere in the middle of nowhere, leaving him with no idea of where to even begin to look at that point.

Before he left to go sort out the rest of his gear, Lieutenant Holton set him up with more magazines for the M4 and the Beretta he'd carried on the lake mission, as well as a large MOLLE pack and a 14-day supply of MREs. He was also given a Gore-Tex parka, gloves and boots and a cold weather sleeping bag. Eric had already seen the first cold front of the season down at that lake, and he knew he'd be facing far worse in the mountains. The rucksack was large enough that he could break the rifle down and stash it inside while in places where he didn't want the attention that would come from looking like he was on combat patrol, but even so, he knew that he had to be ready for whatever he ran into.

When he was taken to the unit where his other gear was stashed, Eric sorted through it to narrow down the essentials. It was in one of his smaller bags that he found a letter from Shauna, expressing her hope that he was alive and would read it soon. She told him what he already knew, that she and Jonathan couldn't wait any longer if they were to have any hope of finding Megan, and she also told him to be sure and check the toolkit he'd assembled for the bikes. It was in that small kit bag that he'd hidden his passport as well, so Eric did, and he smiled at what he found inside. Shauna had hidden three of his one-ounce and two half-ounce Krugerrands in there, knowing that he'd left most of what he had with her and that he might very well somehow loose the few he had with him. How he ever let a woman as smart and thorough as Shauna get away, he still wasn't sure. All he could think of was that he'd simply been an idiot. That had become more self-evident every day he'd been around her in this crisis. He had been concerned until now since he'd blown the gold he had on him on the boat and motor. Like the weapons he carried for fighting, the gold was an essential tool, one that opened doors and options that might otherwise be closed to him.

Just as Lieutenant Holton had promised, Eric landed in Cheyenne, Wyoming that evening. He would have an overnight wait and then the short helicopter flight would carry him on the last leg the next morning. In his conversation with some of the soldiers on the base, he gleaned bits of information about the ongoing operations in the region. Just as was happening in the south, there were terrorist cells that were proving elusive and difficult to contain and destroy, and efforts to do so were limited to the most accessible areas. Given the terrain considerations out here, it was going to take a lot longer to bring this region under control with resources as limited as they were. From what Eric gathered, the Midwest areas he'd flown over that day were among the most secure of anywhere in the nation at this point. The plan was to expand this central command area over time and quell the remaining pockets of resistance, but some of these men that had seen what was happening first hand had their doubts that the country could ever be restored to normalcy. Eric did too, having seen the same thing abroad more than once. Change happened, and then when it was sorted out many of those changes were permanent.

The next morning, he was airborne again at sunrise, staring out in the windows of a Blackhawk at the peaks of the Front Range as they flew south to Boulder. The pilot set the helicopter down at a checkpoint on Interstate 25 east of the city, and from there Eric was driven in a Humvee to the university, which he now learned had been converted into a refugee center. The driver and the other two soldiers accompanying them would wait nearby while he went to the processing building, keeping his weapons and other gear secure in the vehicle until he was ready to leave. Eric had no idea if he'd even be permitted to enter, but when he approached the gates he was carrying nothing but his passport for identification and the coins Shauna had left him, hidden in a small interior pocket he'd sewn inside the front flap of his trousers. The first man he encountered in the processing building was in a foul mood, and clearly uninterested in checking the system for Megan. Their conversation turned heated when Eric wouldn't let up or simply turn around and leave, until they were interrupted by a woman who overheard them through her open office door across the hall.

"Did you say you were looking for Megan Branson, sir?"

Eric spun around to face the woman speaking to him, completely ignoring the irate officer at the desk in front of him. He could scarcely believe his ears, but he knew for certain he'd just heard his daughter's name.

"Come into my office for a moment. I believe I may be able to help you."

Fourteen

WHEN HE HEARD THE woman mention Megan's name and invite him into her office, Eric lost no time going in there. She shut the door behind them and was about to take a seat behind her desk, but Eric stopped her before she had a chance.

"Is Megan Branson here? Do you know her?"

"Are you Eric Branson? Megan's father?"

"Yes! Did she tell you my name? Where is she?"

"No, she didn't tell me. Your wife did."

"Shauna told you? Is she here too? Where are they?" Eric could barely contain his excitement at the thought of an imminent reunion with this family that very day.

"No sir, Mr. Branson. I mean, yes, your wife told me, but no, she's not here, and neither is your daughter, Megan. Your wife and nephew, Jonathan, came here looking for her though."

"Megan's not here? Was she here before? Do you know where she is?"

"No sir. She was never here since the refugee center was established. I have no idea where she is."

"Well, what about my wife? Where did *she* go if she's not here?"

"I'm not sure exactly. When she was here she asked about Megan's friends, and it turned out that one of them is being held here, in the detainment sector. Your wife went in and spoke with her and I think she must have learned something of your daughter from her. They left here to go somewhere else in search of her."

"Who is this girl? I've got to speak with her myself then! I've got to find out everything she knows!"

"Mr. Branson, I went way out on a limb to get your wife inside. It was extremely dangerous to do so and the repercussions for both of us could have been severe if we were found out. I can't do that again."

"Sure, you can! If you did it once, you can do it again!"

"Look, I don't think there's a reason to anyway. Let's just say your wife compensated me for the risk I took. She got her information, and then she said she'd make it worth my while if I'd do her one more favor."

"One more favor? Like what?"

"She told me you might show up here eventually if you were still alive. She asked me if she could leave a letter for you in case you did. She said that you would likewise compensate me in the same way when I delivered it to you."

"What are you saying? You want me to bribe you to give me the letter?"

"No one knows it exists but me. Your wife said you would want it and that you'd gladly give me another one of those shiny South African coins for it. You know, the ones with the pretty antelope on one side? The ones that contain a half-ounce of gold?"

"Or, I could just take it!" Eric said. "It sounds to me like you've been more than compensated for your trouble, Miss Tonya Dale!" He glared back at her face after glancing at her name tag.

"You could try that if you want, sir. Then you might get lucky and get to visit with your daughter's friend in the detention sector after all, but more likely you'll be shot by the guards before you even have a chance to open the envelope. Do you think it's worth it?

Eric continued to glare at her for a moment and then broke into a big smile. He couldn't blame her really. Shauna had already given her gold and promised he'd give her more if he turned up here. She was just taking advantage of an unexpected opportunity like any good capitalist would, and he had to respect that. The gold wasn't worth a damned thing to Eric other than a means to get what he wanted, and right now what he wanted was that letter.

"Okay, you win. Just excuse me a second while I turn around and get it out. Don't worry, the guards have already checked me for weapons, but it just so happens that the last one of those I happen to have is hidden inside my trousers.

"It was in a secret pocket," Eric said, smiling again when he saw the look on her face as she was deciding whether or not the coin he placed on her desk was safe to touch. "Is this what you wanted? Now, can I have that letter? And do you mind if I read it right here before I leave in case I have any questions for you afterwards?"

"Fine with me," she said as she put away the coin and handed over the sealed envelope. "I don't know anything I haven't already told you though."

Eric crossed to the other side of the room and opened Shauna's letter, skimming it quickly once and then reading the words more carefully, he saw that Tonya was right. There was nothing else she could tell him. Of course, he could ask her if she knew anything of the place he now knew that he was going to next, but Shauna had cautioned him not to. She hadn't mentioned Tonya outright, but her words implied that it might be best if the authorities here didn't know where Megan and her friends went. Eric decided she was right; the less anyone knew, the better. The letter was worth far more than its weight in gold, which is what he paid, because now he knew where to look, for both Megan and for Shauna and Jonathan. The date Shauna had written at the top told him how much of a head start the two of them had on him. It was significant, but he knew that the terrain would slow them down if they went all that way on their bikes. Maybe he would catch up before they got there, or maybe not. Either way, it was time to get moving. He thanked Tonya and told her he didn't have any more questions. He left the building and headed down the street to where his ride was waiting a couple blocks away. The two soldiers in the Humvee had orders to drive him here and then to take him back to their headquarters if that's what he wanted but giving him a lift elsewhere wasn't part of the deal. They made that clear when he told them his new destination was west, into the mountains.

"Sorry sir, but that's outside of our AO and off limits to us. We can drop you off a few miles past the edge of town, but that's as far as we can go. I wish we could do more, but I know you understand orders."

Eric assured the driver that he did. Lieutenant Holton had made good on his promise and had delivered Eric to Boulder; he expected nothing more in the way of official help. He had weapons and provisions and a backpack to carry them in, and a destination that he could reach on foot if he had to. But when the other private in the Humvee asked him how far he was planning to go, Eric named the valley that Shauna had described in her letter. He told him that she and Jonathan planned to use the Continental Divide Trail for part of the way as a shortcut and that he figured he'd do the same.

"If they went that way, I sure hope they weren't caught out up there in the high country in that storm."

"What storm?" Eric asked.

"The first real front of the season. What was it, seven, eight days ago?" He asked, turning to his companion.

"Yep, a week ago Monday, wasn't it?"

"Was it a lot of snow? Like a blizzard?" Eric asked.

"Up there? You bet. Not a good place to be for folks that aren't familiar with the weather around here, that's for sure."

Based on Shauna's letter, Eric knew the two of them were likely en route to the ranch at that time. He didn't know how fast they were traveling, but it wasn't fast enough to get that far on the bikes and certainly not on foot if they had to hike part way. He could only hope they were in one of the valleys when the storm hit, and that they found a place to take shelter. Storms like that in the mountains weren't to be taken lightly and could easily prove fatal to the unprepared.

"That route will still be passable now," he continued, as long as you don't get caught by the next storm, but if you're going on foot, you don't want to go the way they went. If you're hiking anyway, there are shortcuts out of the valley here on other trails that'll take you to the divide."

"I don't suppose you have a map?"

"No, not here with me, but I can pretty well sketch out the route from memory. There are National Forest Service trail signs at the major junctions, and most of the trails are well-marked—or at least they were before—but who knows what the vandals out here may have done since? They may have torn all the signposts down, for all I know. But even if you don't have any trouble following the route, it's going to take you days, man. Even using the shortcut."

"Well, if I had a better option, I wouldn't be walking at all, but you guys have your orders and unless you know someone I can hire to take me there, what other choice do I have?"

Eric thought the conversation would end there, but then the driver spoke up. "You could find someone to take you for hire, the problem though, is how are you going to pay for it? Most people are leery of cash right now, and you can't blame them. Things like food and ammo go a lot further, especially on the black market, but if everything you've got is in that pack, you're not carrying enough of anything to trade for a ride like that. Gas is hard to come by, and folks that have it aren't going to burn it unless they've got a damned good reason to go somewhere."

"I'm well aware of the situation regarding cash," Eric said. "And the gas shortage. And yeah, you're right that I'm not carrying enough food or ammo to trade for much, but since I've been back from overseas, I've found there's a lot of interest in an old trading standby that never seems to go out of fashion."

"Oh yeah? And what would that be?"

"Gold."

"Gold?" The soldier laughed. "Yeah, I suppose gold would hold its value in times like these, but who the hell carries gold around with them?"

"I do," Eric said. "So, if you know someone willing to drive me to that ranch, I can give them a solid ounce of the stuff. And in the form of an internationally-recognized coin that is stamped with the content of that particular metal by weight. It was easily worth more than a grand even before the crash, and a lot more now, no doubt." A full Krugerrand was a lot to pay for a ride that should only be a few hours one way, but Eric knew if he had to hike it, he was looking at several days, minimum. And now that he knew where Megan had gone, he didn't care what he had to pay to get there faster. He needed to make sure he arrived before Shauna and Jonathan left with her, as he knew they would if Shauna had her way. He simply didn't have days to spend hiking. And so he made an offer that would get some attention, and it certainly worked.

"A whole ounce of gold? No shit? Man, I think my son will drive you there for that. He's got a four-wheel-drive Toyota truck, and he knows all those backroads. If you're serious, we can stop by and ask him."

"Damned right I'm serious." Eric handed him one of the Krugerrand coins, letting the two of them inspect it closely. When they pulled away from the university, they made a detour off the direct route back to the checkpoint where the soldiers were stationed and turned into an exclusive gated community that was now occupied by security forces and their families. Eric waited in the Humvee with the other soldier while the driver went into the house he'd been assigned to get his son. When they came out, Eric saw that the son wasn't quite the teenaged kid he'd expected, but a young man of perhaps thirty.

"This is Kyle. He's grown up hunting in those mountains where you're going, and he knows the roads. He's got a fuel tank of gas in his Tacoma and jerry cans with more strapped in the bed. He can get you to that ranch today and he's willing to do it for what you said you'd pay."

"Can I have a look at that gold piece?" Kyle asked after Eric introduced himself and shook his hand.

"Sure," Eric handed him the coin. "That's a South African Krugerrand. One ounce of 22-karat gold, guaranteed. I'd say it's a more than enough to cover your expenses and time for a quick jaunt into the mountains."

"There's more to driving around out there than just the time and the fuel. There's a lot of risk in it too. Some folks will kill for a pickup with a full tank these days."

"I don't doubt it. If you're not up for it, I don't blame you. I'll try to find a ride somewhere else."

"No, I'll do it. I'm just telling you like it is. We could run into trouble."

"I've been running into trouble ever since I got back to this country. I'm ready for it. You don't have to worry about the trip on the way out, but if you have a weapon, you'd better bring it. You'll be driving home alone."

"He's not supposed to be carrying weapons as a civilian," Kyle's dad said, but there aren't any checkpoints where you're going and so of course, he will. Kyle's got a Daniel Defense AR and a Sig pistol. He can take care of himself. The main thing is that if you two are going to agree on this, you need to get going now, so he'll have plenty of time to get back here before dark."

Kyle's pickup was equipped with front and rear winches and in addition to extra fuel, he had other emergency supplies and tools stashed in the toolbox and behind the seats. He'd brought a stack of maps out of the house too for Eric to peruse on the ride. They included National Forest Service maps of the Arapaho and Roosevelt National Forests, as well as Continental Divide Trail maps and state maps showing the bigger picture of the location of the ranch that was Eric's destination. After talking with Kyle and seeing all this, Eric didn't have the slightest regret in paying him what he'd offered. And if they reached that ranch and found Megan and Shauna and Jonathan, he already knew he would reward the young man by doubling that. There would still be enough between what he had and what he hoped Shauna was still carrying for them to make their way back to Louisiana, where the rest of his stash was safe aboard *Dreamtime*. But Eric knew it was pointless to plan that far ahead just yet. He was still hours away from that ranch, even with the pickup ride, and he knew anything could happen out there on the road. Naturally, it did.

They were on a gravel forest service road Kyle had taken to cut a significant distance off the trip total, winding up a series of steep switchbacks to a pass over the Continental Divide when disaster struck. Other than a few mule deer and a single black bear crossing the road, they had seen no sign of life up there and certainly no other traffic. But upon the approach to the apex of a blind bend that disappeared ahead around the side of the mountain, Kyle and Eric were suddenly faced with two SUVs barreling downhill towards them at speeds that bordered on suicidal on a road like that one. Kyle was hugging the loose shoulder as far to his side as possible, and in the passenger's seat of the cab, Eric felt as if he were already hanging over the edge of the steep slope that fell away into the canyon to their right. But Kyle had no choice but to try and ease over even farther to avoid a head-on collision, and when he did, Eric felt the right-side wheels drop away as the two SUVs blew by. The Toyota truck began to tip over, seemingly in slow motion, before it rolled sideways down the slope. Both of them were wearing their seatbelts, and Eric had just enough warning to get a good grip on the handle above his door, but there was little else that either of them could do, as gravity was in control now.

Unlike many of the slopes they'd passed on the way up, this one was heavily wooded with closely-spaced conifers, so it wasn't really possible for the truck to roll all the way down to the creek they'd seen hundreds of feet below. Instead, the spruce and fir trees brought it to a stop after one full 360-degree roll and another half turn that left it upside down and smashed against the rocks and tree trunks some 15 feet below the roadway.

Eric glanced at Kyle to check that he was still alive and then braced himself against the top of the cab so he could release his seatbelt. He had bumped his head pretty hard against the pillar, but the aftermarket roll bar Kyle had installed on the pickup prevented the cab from being crushed. Kyle was bleeding from a cut on his face, but considering how much worse it could have been, Eric felt they got off light. He could still hear the SUVs tearing down the mountain road in the distance, the drivers not caring whatsoever that they'd just forced another vehicle off the road.

"Are you okay?" Eric asked. "Anything broken?"

"I don't think so," Kyle said, as Eric cut him free.

The smell of gasoline was overpowering, and Eric remembered the extra fuel cans Kyle had lashed in the back. He reached over and switched off the ignition and then kicked the rest of the broken glass out of the window on his side. There was just enough room to squeeze out next to one of the tree trunks that had stopped their plunge. "Let's clear! I don't like all that spilled gas!"

When they had crawled out with their weapons and moved their other gear to a safe distance, Kyle stared at his wrecked truck and then went into a rage, kicking a tree and cursing the drivers that had done this with every combination of profanity he could recall.

"It looked to me like the vehicle in the rear was chasing the other one. They were oblivious to us or anything else. Otherwise, you'd think they'd have seen what happened and turned around to see if they could help," Eric said.

"Yeah, it was a chase all right. *Assholes!* I didn't have a choice but to move over. We'd probably be dead if either one of them had hit us head-on."

Eric agreed that he'd done the right thing. Both of the SUVs were full-sized. Tahoes or Expeditions or something of that type, though he hadn't been looking for brand emblems at the time.

"My truck's pretty much totaled. But even if it was still drivable, there's no way in hell to get it back up there on the road. Dammit, we're screwed!"

"No, it would take a wrecker with a crane to get it out of there, and you can't just call one up now. But at least we're both uninjured and we can still walk. And we've got our weapons and gear. It could be worse."

"It's going to be a hell of a long walk back home for me," Kyle said.

Eric knew it would be, and he felt bad for him, but what could he do? Kyle had already driven him more than halfway. The Continental Divide Trail crossed this very road at the top of that pass they'd been headed for. Eric had no choice but to keep going until he reached it, and then he would take the trail south until he reached the road that led to the ranch he sought. Kyle would have to set out for home the way they came. If he was lucky, maybe someone would come along and give him a ride all or part of the way.

"I'm sorry about your truck, buddy, I really am," Eric said. "I'll tell you what, though. I was going to give you a bonus if you got me all the way to that ranch. We didn't make it, but you still saved me days of hiking. If you'll give me those trail maps, I'll throw in another Krugerrand. It won't replace your truck, but maybe it'll help you get home."

Fifteen

ERIC REACHED THE HIGH point of the road where it crossed the Continental Divide a little over two hours after leaving the scene of the wreck. It was an unfortunate accident, and even though both of them came out of it relatively unscathed, Eric knew that it put Kyle in a lot of danger, having to walk all that way back home. He was an experienced outdoorsman though, familiar with the area and well-armed, so Eric didn't waste a lot of time worrying about him. He'd paid him double what they'd agreed on, and Kyle was the one behind the wheel when it happened, not Eric. There was little use in speculation as to what the drivers of those SUVs were up to either. They didn't come back while Eric was on the road, so that was all that mattered. Out here, well away from human habitation, he was hiking with the M4 out of his pack and ready for action. But he reached the trail without needing it, and after pausing to study Kyle's maps to make sure of his location, Eric set out to the south on the well-trodden footpath. If Shauna and Jonathan succeeded in what she'd laid out in her letter, then the two of them had passed this

196

way a week or so ahead of him. Eric smiled to himself, thinking about that Florida kid's reaction to this stunning scenery. From the pass he'd left at the road, the trail quickly wound up a ridgeline that fell away thousands of feet on either side, with vistas of jagged, snow-capped peaks as far as the eye could see in the distance. Even down there not far above the pass, there was nearly a foot of snow on the ground in places from the recent storm, and Eric knew more would be coming. In the weeks to come, this high country would be nearly impassable, but the weather was fair and clear now, and if he didn't have any more setbacks, he could make that ranch before the next storm hit.

Although he hadn't seen another person since he left Kyle on that road, Eric stopped often along the trail to look for movement in the distance, especially in the direction where he was headed. There were plenty of places on this trail where it would be easy to run into an ambush, so he had to balance the need to move quickly with the need for reasonable precautions. Moving at night might have been safer in that regard, but now that he was off the roads, he didn't feel that it was necessary. And in this terrain it would be too easy to make a misstep that could cause serious injury, not to mention how much colder it would be after sundown.

Anticipating a frigid night wherever he stopped, Eric made sure that he wasn't on an exposed ridge by the time it started getting dark. He left the trail and descended into a drainage to the east, working his way down into a tall stand of timber until he found a large rock outcrop under which to shelter and where he could build a fire that wouldn't be seen by anyone on the trail above. He kept the fire small and sat close, staring into the flames and thinking about all the things he wanted to ask Megan when he saw her. Mainly, he wanted to ask her forgiveness. He hadn't been there for her, and now he knew her life might have been quite different if he had. Maybe not better, but he could have done a lot more to try and make it so. Daniel had come along and taken his place and had given Megan a lot of the things that money could buy, but he wasn't able to do what Eric was doing now. He couldn't come rescue her here even if he was willing. But Eric knew that if he had been there for her, Megan wouldn't need to be rescued to begin with. And Daniel wouldn't be in the picture at all. He couldn't blame the man for filling the void he'd left with Shauna, because she'd given Eric every opportunity to make it work, but he blew it anyway. And now as he sat there alone in the cold huddled over that tiny source of heat that the high-altitude air seemed to suck away into space, Eric would have traded everything he had and everything he'd ever done to be back in his old home with Shana and Megan, the way it should have been. He sat there thinking these thoughts late into the night, until he finally zipped into his sleeping bag and dozed off, letting the flames die down to coals as he listened to a chorus of coyotes in the distance.

Eric woke before dawn, too cold to sleep any longer despite the high-quality sleeping bag rated for minus ten Fahrenheit. He doubted it was that cold, but he knew those ratings didn't mean a lot either. When he checked the thermometer function on his watch, the reading was actually plus fifteen; certainly cold enough, but it would warm rapidly when the sun came up. Eric rekindled the fire long enough to warm up while he ate an MRE and got his boots on, and then he was packed and moving out at first light. The sunrise over the mountains was spectacular from back atop the ridge top trail, and Eric paused for a minute to appreciate the best part of it. After looking around for signs of other hikers and seeing nothing, he set out again to the south at a brisk pace.

By midmorning, he'd reached a saddle where another trail diverged into a drainage off to the west, and with the sun behind him now, he could see a lone cabin far below in a small, isolated meadow. Horses grazing nearby and smoke from the chimney told him that someone was home, and Eric figured they had a pretty good set-up, their place backing up as it did to millions of acres of national forests and other uninhabited federal lands. Eric knew there were private holdings like that sprinkled throughout the big national forest areas of the West, and from Kyles maps, it appeared that the ranch Megan had headed to was in a similar situation. Eric stared for a moment longer at the tranquil little remote homestead, thinking that whoever owned it was doing quite well compared to what was going on in the rest of the country. He could only hope it was as peaceful at Megan's destination.

It took a full day of hiking to reach the next gravel forest service road that reached the trail, this one dead-ending there at the divide rather than continuing through the pass to the east. After consulting his maps, Eric determined that this was the correct one—the road that would take him where he needed to go. He found a small overhang under a rock ledge nearby to bivouac for the night, and at dawn he was on the move again, this time walking down the rough gravel road that was in reality, every bit as remote as the hiking trail he'd left. There were no signs of tire tracks or other disturbances on the road to indicate recent use. Whether that was good or bad, he didn't know, but he figured folks that lived out here were pretty self-sufficient and unlikely to drive around wasting precious gasoline unless they had a damned good reason to.

Eric followed the deserted road for nearly ten miles. In Shauna's letter, she'd said that Megan's friend told her the ranch was the last one on it before it petered out and ended at the divide trail. Eric didn't know whether the property was on the north or the south side of the road though since the map he had of this area wasn't detailed enough to show individual structures like houses. It did show that the national forest boundary ended at the head of a long valley that headed up a few miles west of the trail though, and he knew he must be nearing it by now that the road was beginning to level out and appeared to be better maintained.

While he would have preferred to survey the ranch from a distance, as he'd done when he spotted the remote cabin yesterday, he doubted he'd get such a view of this one. The road farther up wound through dense spruce and aspen forests with no open overlooks, and now entered the more open ponderosa pines of the lower elevations. When he eventually came to barbed wire cattle fencing on the south side of the road though, he knew he was getting close. Rather than approach the ranch from the road where he might be spotted and seen as a threat, Eric decided to cross the fence and follow it from within the tree line until he saw either the house or drive and could assess the danger. It wouldn't be unreasonable for landowners out here to shoot trespassers on sight, considering all that was going on now, so it was simply prudent to ensure that he saw them before they knew he was there.

Once inside the fence, he expected to see cattle droppings or other signs of livestock, but there was nothing recent, and though he stopped often to listen carefully, he heard no sounds that indicated either domestic animals or human activity nearby. Eric knew that didn't mean much though.

Ranches out here were often vast, and nothing in Shauna's letter indicated the size of this one. Any cattle that might have been in this area could be on a faraway range on another part of the spread, and the house could still be far from earshot. Eric kept working his way west, paralleling the road and fence, knowing he would eventually come to an entrance road leading from the one out front, as there was no other access by vehicle if the maps were to be believed.

He eventually came to a long gravel drive as expected, nearly a mile west of where he'd first crossed the fence. Still having seen or heard nothing to indicate anyone was around, he checked for tire tracks but saw only some faint hoofprints of horses. The drive wound uphill through the pines and open meadows, and Eric kept to cover as much as possible as he followed it, certain that it would lead him to the ranch house. There were more fences to cross along the way, with cattle guards in the drive wherever they crossed. Finally, Eric topped a small rise where he had a view of the home site. There was a barn or stable farther back that was still standing, but the house that had been there was burned to the ground. All that remained was a pile of charred rubble and a stone chimney, along with the blackened body of an older pickup truck that must have been parked in an adjoining garage or carport. Eric's hopes fell as he stared at the scene of ruin before him. If this was the place that had indeed been Megan's destination, then she wasn't here now, and neither was Shauna and Jonathan. He still didn't see any livestock either, and the silence was overwhelming, the land here seemingly as desolate as the mountain wilderness from which he'd just descended. Even so, Eric didn't drop his guard as he approached, moving through the trees and stopping here and there behind the larger ones to look and listen.

When he moved closer to the remains of the house, Eric noticed two nearly identical rock piles in what must have been the backyard. They were the right size and shape to be graves if the bodies were above ground and covered with stones by someone who didn't have the time or means to dig into the rocky ground for a proper burial. Eric studied the other building still standing a couple hundred yards back. He could see that it was indeed a horse barn or stable now. The front gates were open and from where he stood, he could see some of the empty stalls. Keeping the M4 at ready, he approached the rubble of the house to get a closer look. The black soot didn't look like it had been washed by rains since the fire, but there was no heat or smoke either, so it was hard to tell just how recently the house had burned. But when he walked past the rock graves on the way to the barn, he could see that scavengers had gotten to them through the gaps between the stones, partially uncovering them. From the ripe smell of decomposition that was still present, Eric knew they'd probably died around the same time the house had burned, making it unlikely that the fire was an accident, or that the deaths were by natural causes. Someone had survived it though and had taken the time to move the bodies side-by-side, and then gather all those rocks to cover them. But whether that person had been here all along or had arrived afterwards was a mystery.

Eric didn't inspect the graves any closer but instead focused his attention on the barn. He didn't expect to find it occupied after everything else he'd seen here, but perhaps there would be some clue to tell him more about the place. He wasn't convinced now that he was even at the right ranch. It was quite possible that Shauna's directions were inaccurate. After all, the girl who'd given them to her was locked up in that detainment center and had probably never been out here in her life, since it belonged to the grandparents of a friend. He would keep searching the valley until he found someone who could tell him whether or not this was the right place, but he had to assume at the moment that it was not, especially since there was no indication Shauna and Jonathan had been here either.

He reached the front of the barn and pressed close to the rough planking, scanning the dim interior through a large knothole. From there he could see that all of the other stalls were open too, and no animals were present. Other than a pile of loose hay in the back corner, there was nothing else on the ground floor. A built-in wooden ladder leading up to the hayloft over the back half of the barn made it easy to go up there and have a look, so slipping off his backpack, he decided he might as well. A startled rat scurried away behind the bales when his head suddenly appeared at the top of the ladder, but as he poked around up there, Eric was convinced there was nothing else in the old barn, at least until he heard a sudden sound down below, like something big knocking over a leaning board or some other object. Then he heard the sound of footsteps running away on the hard ground outside. It was only seven or so feet from the loft to the ground, so Eric skipped the ladder and leapt down, absorbing the landing in a deep squat and then spinning in the direction of the back gate with his M4 ready to engage.

What he saw nearly caused his heart to stop. A girl in ragged and torn clothing was running for the woods, her long brown hair pulled back in a ponytail bouncing behind her as she went. Eric sprinted out of the barn after her, and as soon as he emerged into the sunlight, shouted at her to stop.

"*MEGAN!* MEGAN STOP!"

At first, he didn't think she heard him, so he shouted again. This time the girl faltered in her stride and hesitated.

"MEGAN! IT'S ALL RIGHT! IT'S YOUR DAD!"

She stopped completely then, and slowly turned around, her eyes wide with fear. That's when Eric saw his mistake. This girl wasn't his daughter, despite the color and length of her hair that was nearly identical to Megan's the last time he saw her. He realized then that he'd wanted it to be her so bad that his mind had made it so, but seeing this stranger's face, he now had no idea who she was. Or he didn't until she spoke:

"You're Megan's dad?"

Sixteen

ERIC LEANED HIS RIFLE against the back of the barn so that he didn't frighten her further and answered the girl's question.

"Yes, I *am* her dad. I'm Eric Branson. Do you know Megan? Is she here?"

The girl hesitated, still unsure if she could trust him, and Eric didn't blame her. She looked traumatized, and he immediately guessed she'd been the one who moved all those rocks. "Megan was supposed to be going to a ranch out here. A ranch that belonged to her roommate's grandparents. Her roommate's name is Vicky." Eric said.

"I'm Vicky," the girl said in a still hesitant voice. "Are you really Megan's father?"

She looked like a frightened deer, caught in the headlights and ready to bolt at the first sign of danger. Eric knew he must have looked scary to her. She'd probably been watching him from the barn as he walked onto the property with his rifle in hand. Now that he studied her closely, he could see bits of hay in her hair and on her clothes, indicating that she had been hiding under the pile of loose hay inside that he'd given little thought to.

"I assure you that I am," he answered. "I came all this way from Europe to find her. I went to the university in Boulder first."

"She told me her dad was some kind of soldier."

"I was," Eric said. "I'm not anymore though." He took a couple of steps in her direction, speaking softly. "Do you know if she is okay? Is she here or somewhere nearby?"

She didn't answer, but she was beginning to relax a bit, so Eric eased closer still talking softly. "Are you okay? Are you hurt, Vicky?"

She shook her head. "No, I'm just hungry. *Really* hungry! I haven't eaten in over a week, I think."

"It's okay. I have food with me. In my backpack."

"Megan's not here. She was, but everyone else left before this happened."

"She left? How long ago?"

"About three weeks, I think."

This wasn't what Eric wanted to hear, but at least he knew Megan had indeed been here at some point, and now maybe Vicky could tell him where she went. It wouldn't do to pressure her though. She was frightened, hungry and had been through no telling what, somehow surviving whatever happened when the ranch house was burned and the two who were buried under those rocks were killed. Eric now

208

figured they were her grandparents. He slowly walked closer until he was halfway to her, and then waited for her to do the rest, which she did. When he took her hand, she suddenly threw her arms around him and buried her face into his shoulder, sobbing, her embrace surprisingly strong for one so famished.

"My grandma and grandpa are dead!" She cried. "They were both so sweet. They would never hurt anyone. They didn't deserve this!"

"This was their place, right? Their house was up there?"

"Yes. Some men burned it. And they shot Grandma and Grandpa. I didn't see it happen, but I couldn't do anything to stop it. I hid in the woods up there on the slope and they never knew I was here. When they left it was too late. Both Grandpa and Grandma were already dead. I couldn't even bury them by myself because the ground here is too hard to dig. I rolled them close together and covered them up with rocks. It was all I could do," Vicky sobbed.

"You survived," Eric said. "That is what they would want for you." He wanted more than anything to ask her to tell him everything she knew about Megan, but Eric knew to wait. The poor girl had been hiding in that barn in terror for days, maybe longer, and he didn't know when she'd last eaten. He held her until she calmed down and relaxed a bit, and then he led her by the hand back where he'd left his backpack in the barn. "Let me get you something to eat. You don't have to be afraid now. You are safe here with me. I won't let anything happen to you."

When Eric had prepared her an MRE entrée of chili with beans, he sat with Vicky as she ate and waited until she was ready to talk some more. "They came and took all the food and my grandpa's guns and everything else they wanted from the house, and then after they shot him and my grandma, they set the house on fire. Then they rounded up all the horses and took them with them too."

"Who were these men, Vicky? Do you know? How did they come here? On the road or on horses of their own?"

"They were on horses. There were a lot of them. I don't know, maybe eight or ten. I have no idea where they came from or why."

Eric wasn't surprised really, after all he'd seen. There were bands of outlaws and raiders everywhere now, and no reason to believe things would be much different here in the mountains. He just hoped like hell that wherever Megan was, she hadn't run into men like that. Vicky was almost finished with her meal, and he couldn't wait any longer to get some more answers.

"Do you know where Megan went, Vicky? And who she was with? Surely, she didn't leave here alone, did she?"

"No, she wasn't alone. She was with Aaron, another friend of ours from the university. She broke up with her boyfriend, Gareth, before we got here, but he was still with us at the time, along with three more of our friends. He wouldn't leave her alone, and he was jealous of her hanging out with Aaron. Aaron wanted her to leave with him because he said he had an even better place to go. I would have gone with them, but I couldn't leave my grandma and grandpa here like that. I knew they needed me, but it didn't matter anyway. Look what happened to them even though I was here!" Vicky began to sob again.

Eric put his hand on hers. "It's okay, Vicky. You stayed here with them. You did the right thing at the time, and it was smart to hide like you did. They would have killed you too. Now tell me, how did Megan and Aaron leave? Were they walking? Do you know where this place is that Aaron wanted to take her?"

"No, they weren't walking. They rode out of here. My grandpa gave them a saddle horse and a pack horse each and supplies too. But they left without telling Gareth. He and one of the other guys were off hunting somewhere else on the ranch. When he got back he was really mad. He yelled at my grandpa and me and everybody else. We didn't know what he was going to do, but two nights later, he and the rest of them stole some of Grandpa's horses and left. I don't know if he was going to try and find Megan or not. He wasn't happy staying out here, but he didn't want to leave without her either. I think that's why she went ahead and left with Aaron first, partly to get away from him and partly to get him away from here and my grandma and grandpa, because he wouldn't leave as long as she was here. He was turning into a real jerk."

Eric couldn't believe what he was hearing. After coming all this way, he just found out his daughter was somewhere out there in these mountains on a horse with just one friend, and possibly a jealous ex-boyfriend in pursuit. And there was another raiding party on horseback willing to kill for anything they could take.

"Aaron is Native American," Vicky said. "He told us that the safest place to go with all that was happening was to his tribal homeland, on the reservation. It's a sovereign nation, or something like that, he said. The people there aren't involved in any of the things that are going on all over America and he said no terrorists or the military or anyone else who didn't belong would bother us there. It sounded good, and Megan believed him. She trusted him."

"An Indian reservation?" Eric asked. "Which one? Do you know what tribe Aaron was from?"

"Yes, Apache. He didn't grow up on the reservation, but he has aunts and uncles and cousins there. But the thing that he said was so good about it was that it's really big, and lots of it is remote, with plenty of places to hide out and people that would take us in because of his family."

"And this is in Colorado?" Eric was thinking most Apaches were originally farther south and west, like in Arizona and Mexico."

"No, it's in New Mexico, but not very far. He said it was just across the state line. I can't remember the name of it. Aaron told us, but it was hard to pronounce."

Eric dug into his backpack and pulled out the stack of maps he'd gotten from Kyle. There was one big roadmap that showed the four states of the Southwest: Colorado, Utah, Arizona and New Mexico. He unfolded it, and sure enough, all the major Indian reservations, as well as national parks and national forests, were outlined on it. "Is this it, do you think? Does that name sound familiar?" Eric pointed as he spoke it: "Jicarilla Apache? Is that Aaron's tribe?"

"Yes! That's definitely the one! I remember it now. I knew the name sounded Spanish."

Eric was relieved that Megan's destination had been identified, but *damn!* That was still a long-ass way, and just when he thought he was so close to her! Northern New Mexico? Could she make it that far, alone with just her one friend on horseback? That ride would be challenging enough in normal times, with weather factors and other dangers of horseback travel in the wilderness. Eric knew their chances of success depended greatly on this Apache friend of hers. He hoped the boy knew his way around horses and the mountains, but his tribal heritage meant little if he'd grown up like most kids these days. And even if he *was* a skilled outdoorsman that could handle such a journey, there were still the other dangers now that required a whole different skill set.

"Your grandfather must have owned a lot of horses," Eric said, "if he gave four to Megan and Aaron and then there were still more for those men to steal after Gareth and his friends stole some too."

"Yes, there were a lot of them. I'm not sure exactly how many. Grandpa loved his horses."

"How many other friends were with Gareth?"

"It was him and three more. Jeremy, Colleen and Brett. Colleen and Brett are a couple. They've been dating since before the riots."

"And Megan was dating Gareth before too? You said he was turning into jerk once you got here. What was going on?"

"Gareth only agreed to come out here because Megan and I wanted to get out of Boulder before things got worse. He did it thinking it was only going to be for a little while, but he kept talking about wanting to go back. He wanted to join the resistance and fight, but we saw some of the things those people were doing, and we didn't want any part of that. It wasn't like we thought in the beginning. It wasn't any kind of peaceful protest. People started getting hurt, and then some were even getting killed, on both sides. And it wasn't easy to tell anymore who was who."

"What is this resistance you speak of? Resistance against what?"

"Resistance against oppression and the police state. They were taking over everything, hurting people with sticks and Tasers and pepper spray and locking people up."

"But they weren't doing this for no reason were they? What started it? Was it the protests that turned into riots? Was it vandalism? Arson?"

"The protests were peaceful until *they* made it violent. Nobody wanted it to turn out like it did, but it got really bad."

Eric had heard enough to get the gist of it. He didn't want to upset Vicky any more than she already was by asking hard questions. The main thing was that she and Megan had enough sense to get away from all that, and Megan had gotten away from this Gareth guy, who sounded like trouble to Eric. "It's okay," he said to her. "I know how these things can happen and turn into something nobody wanted. The main thing is that you got out. How did all of you get here?"

"We hiked. It took a long time, like more than two weeks. We didn't have enough food or anything. Aaron and Gareth tried hunting, but they didn't get anything."

"So, they have guns with them? Did Aaron have one when he left with Megan?"

"Yes, he had one. It wasn't one of those machine guns like yours," she glanced at the M4 propped nearby. "I think he said it was a thirty-thirty? Does that sound right? My Grandpa taught me how to shoot a long time ago, but I didn't really like the noise. I always wanted to ride horses instead when I came here to visit. He taught me a lot about riding, and when we all got here, the rest of my friends learned how to ride too."

Eric was relieved to hear that this Aaron guy Megan had left with at least had a rifle. It would be better if Megan had a pistol too, as she was a pretty good shot the last time he'd worked with her. Vicky said she didn't think she did though when Eric asked. He knew that Megan and Shauna had learned to ride horses after Daniel came into the picture, as he paid for them to join an exclusive equestrian center out in Jupiter Farms where they spent many weekends when Megan was still in high school. That wasn't anything like riding out here in the mountains, but if they had pack animals, Eric knew they were likely moving at a walking pace at best, and hopefully sticking to backcountry trails to avoid the roads as much as possible.

"Aaron said they were going to follow the Continental Divide where they could. There's a route for bicycles too that uses gravel roads and bike trails. He knows to stay away from highways."

After learning all he could about Megan for now, Eric told Vicky that Megan's mom and their friend Jonathan were supposed to be coming here too, and that they might arrive riding bicycles.

"I haven't seen them. No one has come up that road since those men killed my grandma and grandpa. Before that, someone did, but they didn't know this was a dead-end road. It was a man and woman in a pickup truck. They went by but came back after a couple of hours when they got to the dead end. They stopped and talked to Grandpa. They were just lost."

Not knowing were Shauna and Jonathan were was a huge problem now for Eric. He was only here because of Shauna's letter, so he knew this was their destination, but what had taken them so long? They'd had enough time to get here, especially if they had ridden the bicycles most of the way, although Eric knew they could have encountered any number of obstacles or even run into serious trouble, like the kind of trouble that found Vicky's grandparents. The not knowing was a dilemma for Eric, because now he knew Megan had been here and which way she'd headed, but he didn't know if Shauna and Jonathan were still on their way here or if they were never coming. If he went back to search for them the way he'd come, they might arrive by way of the road coming in from the west. And then, there was the problem of what to do with Vicky. Eric couldn't just leave her here, but she was too weak to make a long trek through the mountains on foot with him. She would probably be able to ride, but with the horses gone that wasn't an option. It was already late afternoon now anyway, so he decided maybe it was best to let her eat and rest while he thought about what to do overnight. There was fear in her eyes when she watched him get up from where he'd been sitting with her in the barn, and he knew she thought he was going to leave her.

"I'm not going anywhere right now. I'm just going to go move some more rocks onto your grandparent's graves. I know you did the best you could, but it would be best to put on a few more."

"Thank you. I know you came here looking for Megan and you weren't expecting to find me. I don't want to be a burden to you."

"You're not a burden, Vicky. If I hadn't found you here, I would have no idea what to do next. But I'm not going to leave you. You don't need to worry about that."

The hard work of gathering heavy stones gave Eric time to think about his options, none of which were ideal. Trying to catch up with Megan on foot seemed virtually impossible. Sure, he could hike south to that reservation eventually, but it would take him weeks to do so even alone, and Vicky would slow him down immensely, if she could keep up at all. The two of them could hike back the other way, to the cutoff where Eric had seen that cabin with the horses out front that was obviously inhabited, and he could try to make a deal for some with the gold he had left, but there was no guarantee the owner would be willing to part with something as valuable as horses in times like these. And if both of them left to go back there, Shauna and Jonathan might arrive in the meantime and finding the burned house and the graves, leave before he ever knew they were here. It seemed the only option he had was to leave Vicky here in case they came while he went to see about those horses alone. But he'd promised her he *wouldn't* leave her, and she probably wouldn't trust him to come back if he did. He decided to think about it overnight. He would make camp in the barn and talk to her some more, and then broach the subject in the morning, when a new day would make the prospect more optimistic than the gloom of the long shadows already creeping in as the sun sank behind the ranges to the west.

Vicky had been sleeping in the barn with hay piled around her every night to keep from freezing when the temperatures dropped. She'd been afraid of building a fire because it might be seen, and Eric skipped it too, giving her his sleeping bag when she was ready to turn in and using the hay for himself, which was good enough with the barn walls blocking most of the wind. Vicky looked better in the morning now that she'd regained some of her strength from eating, and Eric decided to go ahead and tell her his plan so he could get moving early. After thinking about it much of the night, there was little else he could do that made any sense.

"Vicky, I promised you I wouldn't go off and leave you, and I won't. But you know I need to find Megan too. I want you to go with me to do that if you're willing to."

"I guess so. I don't know where else I'd go." She had already told Eric that her parents lived in Oregon now.

They'd moved there shortly after she enrolled at the university because her father got a great job offer in Portland. With her grandparents gone, she had no family left in Colorado.

"That's good. I'm glad you're willing to do that. But you know we're going to need horses. I saw a place that had some on my way here, when I was still up on the divide trail. It was about a one-and-a-half-day hike back there, but I can make it in a day if I push it. I need you to be strong for me and wait here in case Megan's mother and our friend Jonathan show up. Can you do that?"

Eric saw the doubt in her eyes, and he took her hand in his and squeezed it firmly. "I'm not going to leave you, Vicky. I promise. I'm going to leave my backpack with most of my gear and food here with you. You can stay hidden in this barn until I come back. I'll be back tomorrow night at the latest, even if I don't get any horses. If I do, it'll be sooner."

"I don't want to be here alone again. I'm so afraid those men will come back."

"There's nothing else here for them to take, and they didn't know you were here. They have no reason to come back, Vicky. But you said you learned how to shoot, right? Have you ever fired a handgun?"

"A little. My grandpa's forty-five."

"Good. I'm going to leave you my pistol. It's even easier to shoot than your grandpa's. You just pull the trigger and you've got seventeen chances to hit what you're aiming at. I don't think you're going to need it, but it'll make you feel better to have it. Can you do this for me, Vicky? So we can go catch up with Megan?"

"I guess so, but please hurry. I don't want to be here alone for long."

Eric gave her another reassuring hug and then quickly sorted out what he could carry, stuffing his trouser and jacket pockets with food, water and a couple of spare mags for the M4. He was traveling as light as he possibly could, counting on reaching that cabin before dark and negotiating with the owner upon arrival. If that failed, he would spend an uncomfortable night somewhere in the wilderness and then return here tomorrow to initiate a Plan B, whatever that may turn out to be.

He struck out up the road at a steady jog, eating up the miles while he could before he reached the steeper terrain of the trail that would slow him down. An hour and a half later, he came to the trail crossing and left the road heading north, stopping briefly at an expansive overlook to catch his breath and replenish his energy with food and drink. When he set out again, he had only been hiking fifteen minutes or so before he heard the unmistakable clop of steel horseshoes on loose rock and the low murmur of human voices. Eric slipped sideways off the trail, ducking behind a pile of large boulders before the riders rounded the bend ahead. He had the M4 in hand and ready, but unless they stopped here for some reason, he didn't expect to be seen from where he watched and waited.

The first rider to come into view wore a cowboy hat and a long duster jacket that made him look as if he would be right at home here in the mid-1800s. The lever-action rifle he carried in a leather scabbard strapped to the saddle completed the picture, as did the loaded packhorse he was leading, burdened by canvas pack bags. There was a second rider following several yards behind, but the first one was nearly adjacent his position before Eric got a look at his companion. This one was leading another horse as well, although it was saddled to ride, rather than laden with packs. Eric stared until the second rider's head finally turned his way, and then he got a good look at the face beneath the green parka hood she was wearing. He had to blink to make sure he wasn't seeing things, but however improbable, he was certain it was her when he called out her name: *"SHAUNA!*

Seventeen

As soon as Shauna and Jonathan had retrieved their weapons they had hidden in the park near the former university campus, they promptly headed west to put the city of Boulder behind them as quickly as possible. The first leg of the journey to the ranch where they hoped to find Megan required riding west on Highway 119, as it was the most direct route into the mountains and to the Continental Divide. After the encounter they'd already had on the bike path, Shauna and Jonathan knew they might run into most anything out there on the road, but it seemed even more dangerous to hang around the deserted streets of the city any longer, as the new refugee center that had been set up at the university seemed to be the only place that was truly secured by the authorities.

"We need to get far enough out of town to find a place to hide, and then wait for dark," Shauna said. Eric had been planning to travel at night when they were all talking about riding the entire way here, and it made sense to do that now too. "It'll probably be really cold riding at night, but I'd rather be cold than be seen."

"Of course," Jonathan said, "The cold's gonna suck, but I'll deal with it. There's no traffic even now, so there's probably nobody driving this highway at night. We'll have it all to ourselves."

"Let's hope so."

The landscape quickly changed as the road began climbing, winding into the smaller hills in the transition zone between the valley and the spine of the Rockies. Shauna had spent a lot of time on a bike over the years, training and competing in triathlons, but riding a loaded bike on seemingly endless uphill grades in the thin mountain air was a different experience altogether. Jonathan was lean and in shape too, but he was struggling at least as much. The only way they could keep the bikes moving on the steeper grades was to shift down and ride at a pace barely faster than walking. Still, it was better than walking, because the bikes were carrying the load of all their gear and supplies, and there would be downhill sections later where they would make up for lost time, at least they hoped. They pulled off on a gravel road to rest and wait once they were well out of town, and though they hadn't yet passed a sign indicating they were in the national forest, the wooded slopes here seemed like wilderness already. Shauna felt better about their prospects of avoiding trouble now that they were in this environment.

Someone on a motorcycle had passed them going the opposite direction before they pulled off the highway, but the rider neither slowed nor waved and clearly didn't want any interaction with them. After dark, when they got moving again, she suggested they try to get off the road and hide whenever they heard a vehicle coming.

"If there's a place to do it," Jonathan said. "We sure couldn't right here."

At the moment he was right. The highway here curved around the shoulder of a mountain with a steep wall of rock just a few feet away to their left, while to the right was a guardrail, beyond which was a drop-off almost steep enough to be considered a cliff. There was nowhere to go if a vehicle approached, and sure enough, one did arrive right at this most inopportune time. They heard the winding of the motor and the shifting of gears long before the headlight beams cut through the dark around the bend behind them. There was simply no way to avoid being seen, so Shauna and Jonathan moved as far to the right as possible and kept peddling. The road was really steep here, and they were barely going five miles per hour. When she dared to glance back, Shauna saw that the approaching vehicle was a big pickup truck, with a livestock trailer in tow behind it. The driver honked the horn as he approached and slowed down to match their crawling speed. Shauna and Jonathan stopped at that point, and she immediately grabbed the Glock from her handlebar bag, planning to have the advantage if this encounter turned threatening in any way. The truck stopped alongside them and in the shadows of the cab, Shauna could see a lone man leaning over to roll down the manual crank window on the passenger's side.

"It's awful cold to be riding bicycles out here in the middle of the night. Where are you two going?"

For some inexplicable reason, Shauna got the feeling that this man could be trusted maybe because he'd trusted them enough to stop when it could be equally dangerous to him too. Maybe it was because he saw that she was a woman, or maybe it was just that they were on such an isolated road at that hour and it wasn't the kind of place troublemakers would seek out. Whatever it was, the feeling was mutual between them, and Shauna told him the name of the valley she and Jonathan were trying to reach. That was a lot farther than he was going, but he offered them a ride to where he was turning off, saying it would save them probably 50 miles of riding. Shauna and Jonathan couldn't express their gratitude enough. At the rate they were going in this terrain, that was *huge*. The man opened his empty cattle trailer and let them put their bikes inside, and then the two of them rode up front in the cab with him.

"Traveling at night is a good idea all right, and that's why I'm doing it too, but I wouldn't want to be doing it on a bicycle. Lots of folks are riding those things now though, all right, and horses too, what with the gas shortages. That's why I've got my trailer back there. I'm on my way home from delivering some horses for the fellow I work for. We're still set for gas for a long time, but who knows how long things will be this way?"

When the Good Samaritan driver, who'd introduced himself as Mr. Stevenson, dropped them off, it was around 2 am in the morning, at the intersection of a gravel forest service road. "Take that road up the top of the next pass. You'll see where the Continental Divide Trail crosses it. You can't miss it. But I'd wait it out 'til morning if I were you. It'll be colder the higher you get, and you won't likely see anybody out here anyway. Once you get on that trail, you'd better try to make good time and get back down out of that high country before you get caught by weather. It's getting the time of year when it can get bad up there. Take my word for it."

"That was a lucky break!" Jonathan said, when the taillights of the truck and trailer disappeared around the bend into the darkness. "I will take his word for the weather too! It already feels like it's 20 degrees colder here than it was back there where he picked us up!"

They took shelter in a dense grove of spruce trees to get out of the wind, getting little sleep before the sun was up and they pushed on towards the top of the pass. The pushing became literal when the gravel road proved much too steep for either of them to pedal on the loaded bikes. "This is why we're going to have to leave them when we reach that trail," Shauna said. "Even the roads here are too steep. The trail will probably be a lot worse."

It took almost the entire day to reach the top of the pass, but they did find the trail crossing right where Mr. Stevenson said it would be. They hid the bikes in the woods well away from it on the off chance that they would need to come back for them, and then set about tying their various small bags and extra clothing and other gear to their day packs. It wasn't the best arrangement for a long hike, but it would have to do. Shauna tucked the Glock into her belt, so it was close at hand and ready, and then they set out to the south, stopping after just a short distance to take in the spectacular view from the spine of a ridge from which they could see for what seemed a hundred miles both to the east and west of the Continental Divide. Jonathan was speechless, having never seen anything remotely like this other than in photos and on television.

But just as Mr. Stevenson had predicted, the weather appeared to be changing by the time they began looking for a sheltered spot among the rocks to spend their first night on the trail. Instead of a starry mountain night, it was dark and overcast and snow flurries were falling as they huddled close to a fire and took turns trying to sleep while the other kept it punched up. By daylight, ominous dark clouds negated any chance they'd be warmed by the sun, and by the time they were hiking the light flurries had turned to big flakes and snow was rapidly accumulating on the trail. After two hours of pushing on to the south through these conditions, the snow was getting much heavier, driven horizontally by biting winds and making it difficult to even see the trail. When they reached a lower saddle between two ridges, Shauna knew they had to find a more sheltered spot to wait out the storm. The trail seemed to lead downhill at a steeper angle here, and the footing was becoming treacherous, with loose rocks hidden from view under the covering of snow. Still, they pushed on, the route dropping fast in elevation, giving Shauna hope that they'd find a warmer place with less exposure to ride it out. Jonathan was ahead of her now, working his way down a slope that didn't seem to have a path at all under the snow, when suddenly, she saw him slip and then tumble and slide. He yelled out as he disappeared from view in the driving snow, and Shauna screamed after him.

She felt her heart racing as she carefully picked her way down to where he'd been standing when he fell. She had no idea if he'd fallen a short distance or gone over the edge of a major cliff until she heard him moaning in pain, his voice barely audible over the howl of the wind. "JONATHAN! WHERE ARE YOU? I'M COMING DOWN THERE!"

Shauna felt carefully with each foot before settling her weight on it as she descended the snow-covered rocks. Some fifteen feet down the slope she saw him, curled in a fetal position where his tumble had been stopped by a small tree. When she finally reached his side, she saw that his lower right leg was bent in an unnatural position, and the look on his face told her he was in excruciating pain.

"My leg! It's broken isn't it, Shauna?"

She already knew that it was, and badly, but she looked down at it again before affirming it.

"Now I'm gonna die out here! That's what happens when you break a leg in the wilderness! I've seen it in too many movies! There's no way I'm getting out of here without help, and there's no one to help!"

"You're not going to die, Jonathan. I know it hurts, but maybe it's not broken all that bad." Shauna knew this wasn't the truth, even as she said it though. The break had to be bad for his leg to be contorted as it was. She carefully pulled his pants leg up enough to make sure there wasn't a bone protruding through the skin, and when she found no blood that was a relief, but even so there was no way Jonathan was walking out of here on his own. He was right when he said an injury like that in a place such as this could result in death, but the more immediate threat to both of them was dying from exposure, and the weather wasn't getting better. Shauna glanced around looking for a place she might drag him to some semblance of shelter, or for branches or something she could use to build one. But something distracted her before she made up her mind which was best. It was something in the air, carried by the wind from somewhere down in the heavily forested drainage below.

"Do you smell that, Jonathan? Is that what I think it is?"

"Woodsmoke," Jonathan said.

"Then that must mean there's someone down there somewhere. It wouldn't be a wildfire in weather like this. At least I don't think so."

"If it *is* somebody, they may not be friendly."

"No, but I've got to try and find out. We've got to have help, Jonathan. I know you're in pain but let me go down there just a little way and see if I can see anything. If I don't, I'll come back and we'll ride out this storm right here and figure out something else when it's over."

Shauna wondered if perhaps the wind was carrying that smoke from somewhere much farther away than she could hope to walk, but she had to try. Leaving most of her gear with Jonathan, she carefully made her way down, finding the going a little easier as she reached the heavier tree cover where the snow hadn't yet accumulated. She turned to look back at Jonathan one more time before she slipped out of sight, knowing the kid was both hurting and frightened, lying there helpless in the middle of nowhere. But the scent of the smoke was still hanging in the air. She followed it on downhill, scanning the trees ahead of her for signs of people, the Glock out and in her hand now that she was on firmer footing and off of those treacherous rocks.

She'd hoped the source of the smoke might be close, but it kept leading her on, down the drainage until she came to the head of a small mountain stream. She wondered if she should turn back, not wanting to leave Jonathan for so long, but what if there was help just a little farther? She had to find out, and so her curiosity took her farther and farther down along the banks of the swift-flowing water until she found stumps of trees that had obviously been felled with an axe. Shauna could tell at a glance the chopping had been recent, too. The cut stumps and the wood chips scattered around them were still bright white and smelled of fresh evergreen sap. Someone had cut them in recent days, and the smoke told her they were still around. She continued quietly on until she came to an opening in the trees overlooking a small meadow farther down. A rustic log cabin stood off to one side of the open area, and not far away a barn that was quite a bit bigger than the cabin. Smoke was pouring out of the chimney, sweeping up the drainage she'd just descended on the bitter cold wind she stood facing.

Shauna hesitated for a few minutes as she studied the remote homestead, then she decided she hadn't come all the way down here just to turn back. She had to take a chance because without help she and Jonathan might die anyway. She tucked her Glock away in her belt and walked into the meadow, calling out loudly as she went, as she didn't want to startle whoever was inside that cabin. She was just a few steps from the front porch when the door opened slightly. A rifle barrel came out first, and then she saw the man behind it. He had an almost white beard, but if not for that, she would have placed him at about her own age.

"I'm sorry to bother you, sir. My nephew and I were caught on the Divide Trail up there when this storm blew in, she turned and pointed back the way she'd come. We were trying to get down off the ridge and find shelter and then he slipped and had a bad fall. He's up there with a broken leg. I smelled the smoke from your chimney and followed it down here."

The man stepped the rest of the way out on the porch, looking Shauna up and down and then scanning the tree line behind her. When his eyes came back to her, they focused on the pistol in her belt. "Put your weapon down and step up here then if you want to talk," he said.

Shauna knew she was taking a big leap of faith to trust this man out here in the middle of nowhere. Once she put that pistol down, she would be at his mercy, but even if she didn't he already had the drop on her. She had committed herself when she approached his cabin. She did as he asked, and to her relief, he lowered his rifle, leaning it against the door casing as he stepped forward to offer his hand.

"Bob Barham," he said, as she accepted his handshake and introduced herself as well. "That ridge up there is no place to be in this weather," Bob said. "Why don't you go in there and warm up by the fire. There's coffee on the stove. I'll go saddle three of the horses. Can you ride? Can your nephew?"

"Yes!" Shauna said. She hadn't even considered that this man might have horses. Until he mentioned it, she had no idea how they might get Jonathan down here even if he agreed to help. but horses would work! She didn't know if Jonathan had ever even been on one before, but she would make it work if Bob was willing to do this for them. "Can the horses make it up there in this weather?"

"Oh yeah, as long as we don't wait to get going. It's going to get a lot worse before it gets better, but we've got time to go get him and get back down here. We'll have to lead them the last little bit where it gets steep, but if we can get him mounted he can ride all the way down. Is it a bad break?"

Shauna assured him that it was. He needed to go a hospital, but she didn't see a vehicle parked on the place and didn't know if that was even possible. When Bob left for the barn, she looked around the interior of the small cabin and it was clear to her that Bob lived there alone. It was also clear that he had a fascination with all things pertaining to the frontier West, just as the outside of the cabin had suggested at first sight. The walls were hung with mountain man and Native American art and collectibles, including antique flintlock rifles, bows and arrows and other weapons. While there wasn't a woman's touch in evidence anywhere in the decor, there were several photos of a pretty woman about Bob's age that suggested he'd had a wife once and was possibly a widower now. Shauna knew she'd made the right choice to take a chance here and had an intuitive feeling she could trust this man. Before he'd left her to go to the barn, Bob had picked up her pistol from the snow where she'd set it down, wiping it dry before handing it back to her. He believed her story too and he genuinely wanted to help, and she supposed it was because he was living so remotely out here. Although there was a rough, unpaved road leading to the cabin from somewhere, there wasn't a vehicle in sight and it appeared he was living here without the convenience of one. From looking around inside the cabin, she was sure that's how he wanted it, and maybe because of that, he'd avoided the nastier elements of society that she'd unfortunately had so much experience with already.

"Help yourself to those biscuits too," Bob said when he returned to the cabin and uncovered a pan with several fresh ones in it. "Have you two been eating? Are you carrying supplies?"

"We have MREs. That's about it, though."

"That's not food! When we get your nephew back down here I'll feed you both properly. You can tell me how you came across the MREs and the rest of your story on the ride up there. Are you ready to go?"

Shauna grabbed two of the biscuits and followed him out. The horses were hitched to the porch rail, seemingly unperturbed by the snow and cold. She didn't have to tell Bob how to get up there. He used that route up the drainage to reach the Divide Trail quite frequently. Shauna called out Jonathan's name when they drew close, just so he wouldn't be startled by the sight of the three horses and start shooting at them with that little .380. Getting him up the saddle was an effort, and he screamed in pain when Bob accidentally bumped his leg, but they soon got him down the mountain and into the warmth of Bob's cabin.

"It's a long way to any place we might find a doctor son, even if it weren't for this weather. If you want that leg to heal to where you can walk again, you're going to have to be tough and let us set it back in place. It's not as bad as it looks, but you can't leave it like that."

"Is it gonna hurt more than it does now?" Jonathan asked.

"Yep, but the worst of it won't be but a few seconds. You can drink all the Jack Daniels you want before we start. It'll help."

"I feel like I've gone back in time," Jonathan muttered. "Am I living in a Western movie now or what?"

"It's going to be okay, Jonathan," Shauna said. "We're really lucky that we found help so close to the trail. Bob told me he was a medic in the Army at one time. He knows what he's doing."

"I wasn't in long," Bob said. "And I wasn't much older than you when I was, but she's right. I got all the medic training even though I never shipped overseas or anything like that. I might have forgotten most of it, but it'll come back to me," he grinned, taking a swig of the whiskey himself. "We'll get you fixed up so that leg will heal and then you two can be on your way as soon as you feel up to it."

* * *

More than a week passed after the day Jonathan broke his leg and Shauna was starting to feel trapped again, cooped up as she was in Bob's little cabin, still worried about Megan, her plans to reach that ranch thwarted by the kid's accident. There was no telling when Jonathan would be able to hike again, but after all that waiting, Bob agreed to leave him there and to take Shauna to that ranch to see if they could find Megan. Bob said the trail they'd been on was indeed the shortest route, and that they could get there on horseback. When they left, they took an extra saddle horse for Megan to ride back on if they found her. They had only been on the trail a couple of hours and Shauna was bursting with excitement at the prospect of seeing her daughter when she was suddenly startled by a voice calling her name from seemingly out of nowhere. At first, she thought she was simply hearing things, but when she saw how it startled the horses and caused Bob to reach for the rifle in his scabbard, she knew it wasn't just her imagination.

"Shauna! It's me, Eric!"

It made no sense at all, but that voice was unmistakable. She told Bob it was okay, and a moment later Eric Branson stepped into view from out behind a jumble of boulders next to the trail.

"Eric!" Shauna swung down from the saddle and handed the reins to Bob, who was putting two and two together after all Shauna had told him about her ex-husband. Shauna threw herself into Eric's arms and he pulled her close to him. "Lieutenant Holton said you were dead. I never believed it, Eric! But how did you find me here? Did you go to the university first?"

Eric told her that he did, and that he got her letter and that he'd already been to the ranch and that Megan wasn't there. He told her what happened to Vicky's grandparents and the ranch house, as well as the horses, and how Vicky was waiting there right now for him to return.

"We were just going there to see if Megan was there," Shauna said. "That's why we have an extra saddle horse. I was so hopeful that she would be there and that we could bring her back." Then she told him what happened to Jonathan, and how they'd been waiting in Bob's cabin for days for the conditions to improve so they could make the trip to that ranch.

"It sounds like he's in a good place then," Eric said. "Vicky, on the other hand, is traumatized, as you can imagine. I hated to leave her alone there at all, but she was too weak to keep up. Horses are exactly what I had in mind when I left there this morning." Eric reached up and patted the mare she was riding.

When Eric told them of the place he'd spotted from afar on his way out to the ranch, and that he had been heading back there to see about finding some horses, Bob just grinned. It was his own place, visible from an overlook at one specific point along the main trail. Shauna and Jonathan hadn't been able to see it that day in the snowstorm, but Bob had pointed it out to her this morning when they rode up out of the drainage. "We can go on over there right now then and get her," Bob said. "She can ride back on the packhorse or double up with one of us. We'll take her back to my cabin so she can get her strength back, and then all of you can figure out what you want to do."

"You are too kind, Bob," Shauna said. "We sure haven't run into many folks as helpful as you."

Bob shrugged it off and led the way, riding on ahead so Shauna and Eric could talk and catch up on everything that had happened since the two of them last saw each other. The news Eric learned of Megan from Vicky didn't do much to ease Shauna's worries though.

"At least we know where she's heading," Eric said. "And she's with someone who supposedly knows this country if what Vicky said is true."

"But how far is it to New Mexico from here, Eric? And how will we get there?"

"Maybe the same way she is; horses? Do you think Bob would be willing to part with any of these? How many more does he have?"

"A few more, but I doubt he'll sell. From what I know about him after being around him for over a week, I'll bet he'll let us use them for free though if we let him go with us!"

About the Author

SCOTT B. WILLIAMS HAS been writing about his adventures for more than twenty-five years. His published work includes dozens of magazine articles and twenty-two books, with more projects currently underway. His interest in backpacking, sea kayaking and sailing small boats to remote places led him to pursue the wilderness survival skills that he has written about in his popular survival nonfiction books such as *Bug Out: The Complete Plan for Escaping a Catastrophic Disaster Before It's Too Late.* He has also authored travel narratives such as *On Island Time: Kayaking the Caribbean,* an account of his two-year solo kayaking journey through the islands. With the release of *The Pulse* in 2012, Scott moved into writing fiction and has written several more novels with many more in the works. To learn more about his upcoming books, sign up for his mailing list or contact Scott, visit his website: www.scottbwilliams.com

Made in the USA
Middletown, DE
18 October 2018